Olivia

Shayna Astor

Edited by NiceGirlNaughtyEdits

Edited by Beth Hudson

Cover Designer Fine's Fine Designs

Formatting Fine's Fine Designs

Olivia

Copyright © 2023 Shayna Astor

From the Author

Olivia is a full-length, novel that features strong language, mature situations, explicit sexual scenes, alcohol use, mentions of death, grieving, and a car accident. This book is intended for readers age 18 and up.

While Olivia can be read as a stand alone, it is recommended to read the series in order.

Thank you so much for reading my novel! I hope you enjoy reading it, as much as I enjoyed writing it!

Other Books by Shayna Astor

Hot & Cold

Shattered Pieces

Own Me (A dark romance)

Off Limits (Book 1 in the Limits Series)

Love Me Not

Faking Perfection: A Brighton High School Reunion

Dedication

For all the opposites who attract.

Chapter 1
Liv

The lunch rush is always my favorite time of day. People bustling in to get their midday caffeine fix or a quick snack, usually both. The hustle keeps me going, gives me life.

That's why the lull we're in right now is almost boring me to tears. People watching is a pastime of mine, and there's no better place to do that than the large windows in the front of the shop. This time of day is always guaranteed to provide some good entertainment. It's not busy, but I can take more in, truly observe my sleepy town of Juniper Grove, New York, that I both love to hate, and hate to love.

"Anything good today?" Alina bumps her hip into mine as she rests her forearms on the counter.

"Mrs. Henderson just walked into the pharmacy." I don't veer my eyes from the picture window as I answer her.

"Ah, so we have about ten minutes until the shouting begins."

"Roughly." Pulling my attention from the world outside our quaint little shop, I turn to my sister. "You look tired, Leen."

"I'm fine. Early mornings and all that." She waves me off like it's nothing, but I know she hasn't been sleeping well. She thinks I can't hear when a nightmare wakes her up screaming at three in the morning. My room is only down the hall; I don't know what she expects.

"Leen, stop lying to me. You're having nightmares again. You promised me next time, you'd see somebody." It's not just the middle of the night screaming that tips me off. It's the fact that she's been staying at my house at all. We have our own houses, yet she insists on staying with me most nights lately, claiming she wants more sisterly bonding time.

Stiffening and taking a step back, she wipes her hands on her apron, which I'm sure only gets them more covered with flour. "I'm fine."

"You're *not*. Please, for me." When I reach out to touch her shoulder, she shrugs me off.

"I'll think about it. I'm going back to the kitchen. Any requests for the afternoon?"

Huffing out a breath, I move on. I know it won't make a lick of difference what I say or do. We've been here at least a dozen times in just the past two years.

"Some of those mixed berry muffins would be great." Defeat hangs off my words and slumps my shoulders as I force a smile.

The smile she plasters on her face makes it all worth it, though. "You got it."

Grabbing a rag, I start wiping down the tables, gathering the few tips left behind from the rush I had yet to clear.

While focusing on the last table, scrubbing at something sticky that the cute, but loud, blond toddler left behind, the bell chimes.

A boisterous voice fills the otherwise silent café, and immediately I'm put on alert.

"I don't know what kind of backwards, one-horse town I arrived at this morning, but this is going to be a long trip. No, the motel is horrendous."

Glancing over, I see a grade-A prick, in what is clearly a very expensive suit, with its sharp lines and the way it's tailor fit to his body. There's a phone plastered to his ear to complete the too-busy-for-you image. Despite overhearing his conversation, I'd peg him as a visitor from the first second. Aside from never having seen him before, and knowing everybody in this Godforsaken town, he sticks out like a sore thumb. We're not a suit and dress type of area.

Hands spread in front of me, I stand behind the counter, ready to take on this suit.

"Yeah, I'm going to go, see if I can get at least a halfway decent cup of coffee here." He hangs up without so much as a goodbye.

"Hi, how can I help you today?" The smile stretching my lips couldn't be more fake, but it's all about impressing the customers. That's what my other sister, Mazie, always says, at least, when she reminds me that I'm the face of the store. Whose brilliant idea that was, I have no idea.

A curt smile is returned to me. "I'll have an espresso macchiato with three shots of espresso. You know how to make that, Sweetheart? It requires the fancy machine over there." He points to the espresso machine, like I've never seen one before. Except for the fact that I've been working here for over three years and read the handbook cover to cover. Twice.

"Oh, you mean this thing? Here?" I walk over to the espresso machine like it's a foreign object. "Hm, it sure does have a lot of buttons and levers. I'm not sure. Maybe you can order something else? Like a plain coffee. I think I can make that just fine." I use my most innocent and naive sounding voice, letting him think I'm just some stupid bimbo.

"Maybe they should hire somebody who knows how to use the machinery. Somebody smart enough to figure it out," he grumbles.

Normally, I'd let it go and make his drink. But he's pushing all my buttons in all the wrong ways. With the sweetest smile I can conjure, I break the news. "Actually, we don't have espresso macchiatos here."

One of his eyebrows arches. "Excuse me?"

With one finger, I point to the chalkboard sign above my head. "I think what you're referring to is a Diva Espresso."

"Yeah. I'm not saying that."

"Then I'm afraid I can't help you."

"Seriously?"

I shrug and step back. "It's what's available on the menu."

"Why would you even call it something like that?" He sounds utterly revolted by our choice of title.

"Because it's a drink only ordered by divas," I retort without batting an eyelash.

His hands plant on his hips before he waves one in my direction. "Fine. I'll have that."

An evil grin snakes across my face. "Sorry, but I'm going to need to hear you say it."

He stares at me blankly for a minute and I'm not sure he's actually going to do it. But he sighs heavily, bringing his fingers to pinch the bridge of his nose. "One Diva Espresso. Fucking small-town nonsense," he mutters the last part under his breath.

I suck my teeth and grab a large cup, bigger than he asked for, but I'll throw in the extra for what I'm about to do. Scribbling on the cup, I turn my back and set to making his drink. My focus will ensure it's the best damn one I've ever made.

I feel his eyes on me and glance over my shoulder, just long enough to catch him staring at my ass. Rolling my eyes, I give my head a shake. We have a pretty busy tourist business here, so I'm used to newbies coming in, hanging out, and chatting me up. But this guy? He screams *asshole*.

Sliding the cup over the counter toward him, I bend forward, squeezing my chest a touch so my cleavage is on point. When his eyes drop, I all but jump up and down. Teasing rich assholes is something I excel at. It gets me free drinks at the bars in Pineville City, only a half hour away, all the time.

"I hope it's to your liking." I put on the sugariest voice and smile I can muster. "Oh, and also, it's not polite to check out your barista."

"Excuse me?"

"Please, I saw you, checking out my ass, looking down my shirt."

"Maybe don't throw yourself across the counter and I won't look down your shirt. Or dress more professionally in your place of business."

Standing in front of the register, I quickly ring him up. "That'll be three seventy-five. Unless there's anything else?"

His eyes roam the clear case to the right. "A muffin."

The mixed berry aren't out yet, though I can smell that they're almost done. Good thing, because this guy doesn't deserve one. Instead, I grab a coffee crumb and put it in a bag.

"Five sixty."

"Does this place even take credit?"

"Of course we do. All major companies." My faux sweetness is wavering.

As he lifts his cup to take the first sip, I watch as his eyes drift to the two letters I scribbled at the top. "DB?"

"Yeah, for douchebag. That is your name, isn't it?" My eyebrows perch high on my forehead.

His lips press into a line as his eyes narrow. "I'd like to speak to your manager."

Tapping my fingers on the counter, I step back and point briefly at him. "Sure thing, I'll go get her."

As I walk away, pride swells in my chest as I hear the faintest "mm" from him. Whipping off my apron as I walk through the door of the kitchen, I toss it on the table in the middle of the room.

"Tough customer?"

"Oh, you know, just another guy who thinks he's hot shit."

"You got it?"

"You know it."

Squaring my shoulders, I walk back out, a Mazie smile plastered on my face.

"Hello, sir, I heard you'd like to speak to a manager. What can I help you with?"

"You have got to be fucking kidding me. There's no way you're a manager here. You're what, twelve?" His gaze tracks down and back up my body.

"I'm twenty-three, thank you very much. See that 'Three Sticks' on the sign? I'm one of the three. My sisters and I own the café and bakery. I'd be happy to get one of them for you if my service is not to your liking."

Grumbling incoherently, he spins on his heel and walks toward the door.

Resting one elbow on the counter, I wiggle my fingers. "Thank you for your patronage. Please come again."

When he walks out, I bang my head against the wood in front of me. I love our shop, I love my sisters, but I hate this job.

The warm scent of lemon zest wafts into my nose and I turn my face just enough to see a fresh-out-of-the-oven mixed berry muffin in front of me.

"Your favorite, Sibby."

Taking a big bite, I don't even try to stifle the moan. My sister is an amazing chef. "You know I hate that name," I mumble around a mouthful of food.

"I know. But I love it." Alina is only two years older than I am. When we were little, she couldn't quite say "baby sister," so it came out as "Sibby." The nickname has stuck around for twenty-three years, and at this rate, I'm sure I'll never be rid of it.

"Only for you, Leen." I tilt my head to the side to rest my head against hers. While I may have the crazy colored hair and fashion flair–as Mazie likes to put it–Alina and I aren't all that different. Both a little more independent, both a little more on the wild side, but both fiercely family oriented.

Chapter 2
Jameson

I can't believe the girl with hot pink streaks in her hair not only works at the café but is one of the owners. What fucking luck.

Not only that, but since my first encounter there three days ago, I haven't been able to get her out of my head. Or find a halfway decent cup of coffee. As much as I hate to admit it, their coffee is really damn good, as was the muffin.

The biggest thing clogging up my mind is that girl. Her hot pink streaks flutter through my thoughts, I can almost feel the rips in her jeans under my palms, and the jingle of her armful of bangles filters through my dreams.

One encounter. I've had one encounter with her. She's young, practically a baby, small town, and very much the opposite of me. The hair coloring and attire are highly unprofessional and surely a sign that she's lacking drive and desire, possibly even brain cells. But she's the most gorgeous woman I've ever seen. Who would've thought I'd run into someone so distracting in a town so tiny. I mean there's only one stoplight in the whole damn place.

In the past few days, I've met my fair share of townies, mostly as I'm stuck walking down the block behind them. Everybody walks so damn slow here. Like they're tourists in the city who have to take in every building. It's infuriating. We walk fast in Manhattan. Always somewhere to go, somewhere more important to be.

The fact that I have to go back to Three Sticks Bakery and Café is both worrisome and exciting. It should be neither. I've been self-employed for six years and never once have I had an issue getting involved with the community or its members. I keep to myself, stay around the hotel and job site. That's it.

Every so often when things get stale, I'll go to a bar or nightclub. Getting a quick hookup in is usually easy since I'll be gone within weeks. There are no strings, no chance for anything real, and I make sure that's known from the second we say hello. I enjoy single life far too much to get weighed down, especially in a faraway town.

Get in, get out. That's my motto with my job.

This time will be no different. It can't be.

"So, what do people do for fun around here?" It's not a question I usually ask, but this motel has far less to do than most places I stay.

I'm here, in the tiny town of Juniper Grove, to fix the supermarket, Shop Mart. They're hemorrhaging money and resources and called me in to help, because I'm the best at what I do. Which is work on the books, as well as every other aspect of their business, and figure out how they can change to be more conducive to staying in the black. If they can't, if I can't help him out, then the store closes and everybody loses. I do my best to keep that from happening.

"Most people drive to the city about a half hour west. Big bar scene, some clubs, restaurants more than just chains and the diner. Easy to walk around too."

Seth's a nice enough guy. I hope I can help him out and right his sinking ship. It's harder to shut down a big business like this one when the manager's actually a decent human who cares about his employees.

"Not much here. It's probably the smallest town I've been to." The words come out absentmindedly as I look through some papers.

"Yeah, it was built around a plant years ago. Like most areas, it built up, became a bit more populated. But once the plant shut down, expansion stopped. We have a pretty good tourist turnout, though. Lots of festivals and whatnot."

"That sounds..." Dreadful. But I can't say that. How can this town be good for tourism? I guess it's right off the highway, and the downtown area is pretty bustling with kitschy shops and small boutiques.

"Oh, it's awful. Fun for the kids, great for the town, but being a resident who has been to his fair share, they're pretty repetitive. Been to one, been to them all." He leans back in his chair and kicks his feet on the desk.

"And the coffee? Not much from what I've seen so far." My eyes lift over the forms still in my hand.

"Nah, not really. The diner isn't too terrible, but outside of that, if you don't want to drive twenty minutes for Starbucks, the best you'll get is Three Sticks. It's actually really good. They bake all their own pastries too. Those Baker girls." He crosses his arms across his stomach and shakes his head. "They've been through a lot. I'm glad they've been able to turn things around. You been in there yet?"

"I have, in fact. Don't think the girl out front liked me too much."

"Ah, so you've met baby Baker. That one's a firecracker, I'll tell ya." His gaze lifts to the ceiling, almost as though he's replaying a scene or two in his mind.

"I saw that firsthand. She wrote DB on my cup. Told me it stood for douchebag."

Seth leans so far back in his chair, his head tipped to the ceiling as he guffaws, that I'm afraid he may actually fall over backward. "Man, I'm sorry, that's just too much like her."

"Little rude, don't you think? Especially being a proprietor?"

He shrugs and looks me dead in the eye. "Did you deserve it?"

Adjusting my feet, I cross the left over the right as I continue to lean against his desk. "I guess I did. I wasn't exactly polite. I'd just gotten to town and was running late. Plus, small towns, they're not really my thing."

"That girl has always been bigger than this town. But she'll never leave."

My brows bunch together, and I put down the papers and cross my arms over my chest. "Why not?"

Seth flips his chair straight, leaning over his paperwork again. "Not my business to tell. But know that those girls have been through more than you can imagine." The serious look on his face and hardness of his eyes tells me to drop it.

Clearing my throat, I gesture toward the papers spread on Seth's desk. "Able to make heads or tails of what you got there?"

"Just trying to gather what you've asked for. It's a little intimidating, and terrifying, knowing that the life of this company rests in your hands."

"I'm very good at my job, Seth. It's why you hired me." I lay a hand on his shoulder. It's supposed to be comforting, but I'm not always sure it is.

"We just...we all lose a lot if we shut down. The whole town."

"Shutting a business down is not something I take lightly, and it's always my last resort. I promise to do my best to get you on your feet, set you on the right track, and try my damndest to keep you open."

It's what I always do, but I work a little harder and a little longer when I like the business owner, and Seth is a nice guy with a big heart.

I can tell from the way he greets his customers by name. The care he takes with the groceries. The way he'll step in if they're shorthanded or just to be helpful. And he has a smile on his face any time he's on the floor, even if it drops the second he's behind his office door.

"I appreciate that, Jameson."

"Call me Jay. Please."

He nods resolutely as he goes back to his papers.

"I'm going to leave you to keep rifling through, if you don't mind. I plan to grab a cup of coffee. You want one?"

His head shakes, but he doesn't lift his gaze. "No thanks, I'm anxious enough as it is."

"Don't be. We'll fix this."

A quick pat on his back and I grab my sport coat. Guess it's time to revisit the girl with the pink streaks who runs through my mind on repeat.

Chapter 3
Liv

It's been almost a week since Suit first walked in and, thankfully, he hasn't been back. I've heard rumblings that he's here for work and have seen him around town, but I haven't had to have another encounter.

Until today, when he walks in after the lunch rush.

This time, though still dressed in what appears to be an expensive suit, he doesn't have the phone pressed to his ear. His coat is open, revealing a light blue shirt that fits far too perfectly against his taut chest and tapered waist.

I hate myself for noticing. He's so the opposite of my type, and I have no want to develop even an inkling of a crush on this man.

With his hands shoved in his pants pockets, he walks straight up to the counter and looks at the baked goods we have before his gaze lands directly on my chest.

"What the fuck are you doing, perv? Stop checking out my rack." I turn my body and back away.

"I'm looking for a damn name tag, Jesus." His voice holds nothing but irritation.

Crossing my arms across my chest all the same, the fire inside me douses a little. "Oh. Wait, why?"

"I'm curious as to what your name is, obviously. I'll be coming in here for a while, and it'd be nice to be able to call you by your name instead of 'girl with pink hair' or 'that barista.'"

"Coming in regularly, huh? Why is that?" As much as I don't want to be, I'm intrigued.

"You have the best coffee in town. And that espresso macchiato was one of the best I've had."

"So, I guess I do know how to work that big fancy machine thing." Resting my forearms on the counter, I lean forward, giving him a full view of my cleavage, while I work the rag between my hands.

To Suit's credit, his eyes don't leave mine, though his taut jaw does make it seem as though he's fighting the urge to glance lower.

Standing straight, I point over my shoulder toward the espresso maker. "Want another one?"

"That'd be great."

Turning my back to him, I grab a cup and start brewing the espresso. "This going to be a regular drink for you?" I ask over my shoulder.

"Could be. You make a damn good one."

We stay silent while I finish making his coffee, adding a lid. Spinning back around, I slide the cup across the counter. I stifle a laugh as he holds it up and examines the name I gave him this time.

"Suit?"

"Yeah, cause..." I gesture my hand up and down his frame.

One corner of his mouth tips down. "You could just ask my name, you know."

"I'd have to care. And I don't." Nope. Definitely don't care about this gorgeous specimen of a man's name. As he's gotten closer, I've noticed his eyes are almost silver and contrast perfectly against his dark hair.

"You may want to learn it. Like I said, I'll be in here a lot, probably at least once a day. I need a lot of caffeine to function with my job." He seems very interested in me knowing his name.

"And you'll be in town for a while?" I wipe a rag across the counter, cleaning off imaginary crumbs.

He takes a sip and tilts his cup toward me. "Could be a few weeks to a few months."

"What are you doing here, exactly?" Curiosity is getting the better of me. I need to be careful before I turn out like the cat.

"I'm here to help Seth Plienne keep his business open."

I straighten my spine, completely stiff, as I meet his gaze, hardening my own. "You better not fuck with the Plienne's. They're a Goddamn institution. And their grocery store employs more people than any other business in this town."

"Seems your family is a bit of an institution itself."

My teeth clamp together, and all the blood in my body freezes. "Don't talk about my family. To anybody. Got it?"

"I'm sorry, I didn't mean to—" He at least looks genuinely sorry.

"Just don't. You should go. Every Wednesday afternoon, we have a group from the high school come in. They'll be here any minute." I take a step back from the counter, away from him.

When he looks at me with his mouth slightly agape, head turned to the side a bit, I know he's wondering about my sudden change in demeanor. Maybe if he sticks around long enough, or listens, he'll learn you don't bring up the word 'family' to the Bakers. Sisters? Sure. Siblings? No problem. But family? That's the F-word in our foursome. We don't utter its existence.

"Uh, okay. I'll be in tomorrow."

"Sure thing. Come again."

With one more quick look back, he's out the door, sliding a hand into his expensive suit pants pocket and heading up the street toward the grocery store.

Chapter 4

Jameson

There's definitely some sort of dark cloud surrounding the Baker family. The way baby Baker reacted was nothing short of shutting down. I wish I knew her name, I'd much prefer to think about her by that rather than "baby Baker."

Fuck. I don't want to be thinking about her at all.

If she keeps making my coffee like this, though, there's no way I won't. Plus, she banters nicely. Verbal sparring matches are always something I'm up for. It doesn't happen too often with quick hookups. Especially when they aren't any smarter than the bubblegum they're popping.

But baby Baker seems different. The way she talks and holds herself, she's smarter than most. She told me that first day that she's twenty-three, which puts her at seven years younger than me. Not something I'm into.

None of it should matter, as I keep my time in these towns short, sweet, and uncomplicated. A woman certainly muddles things. Especially when she's more than a possible quick hookup. And I can tell, even though I don't know her first name, baby Baker would be far more, because I already can't stop thinking about her.

If I got to taste her? To feel her? To hear what she sounds like while I'm deep inside her. Well…I'd probably never get her out of my mind.

So instead, I have to keep this professional. I'm a patron of her café, and it has to be just that. It has to stay that way.

I can't let things become complicated. No part of me wants to get married or have kids, and if some girl becomes too close…well, I've yet to find a woman who doesn't want to settle down.

It's entirely possible that we'd be able to have what would surely be mind-blowing sex and then move on with our lives, but I'm not prepared to find out.

So, baby Baker is going to remain my source of coffee and nothing more.

Chapter 5
Liv

"No! Please. Not this." The voice echoes all the way down the hall.

I'm out of bed and running before I have a chance to think, my mind and body heavy with sleep.

Alina is in the guest room, just a few feet down the hall from my bedroom. She's tossing and turning, and I get to her just as she opens her mouth for what I know will be an ear-splitting scream. I've experienced this too many times not to.

"Leen. Sissy, it's me." I loop some brown and pink curls behind my ear and bend down to touch her shoulder.

"Alina." I shake her this time, but she's still tossing and whimpering.

With a heavy sigh, I sit on the edge of the bed and drop my head in my hands. I'd be somewhat embarrassed about being in my panties and a tank top if she wasn't my sister and best friend.

She finally stills without waking, no more crying.

"Alina, I love you, but I can't keep doing this. We need to at least tell Mazie, or Eli." She has no interest in telling our older brother and sister. They know she used to have nightmares. They don't know they've returned. And with a vengeance.

It makes sense. With everything we've been through, anybody could have horrible dreams. I know I have. Mazie and Eli each function in their own way.

But Alina seems to get the brunt of it, and they haunt her. Part of it is because of her ex-boyfriend, Cameron, and how and when he left her. He had been part of what held her together after the event.

That's one thing about us. We don't talk about it in specifics, we don't refer to it as anything other than *the event*. And we don't need to, because it changed our lives and our trajectories. It changed everything.

The whole town knows, and they know not to bring it up, which is why it shook me so much when Suit mentioned it today. How he could know anything is beyond me.

Seth must be talking, but what is he saying?

It seems Alina is dreaming about something else now, because she laughs, and a smile breaks across her face, causing one to stretch across mine. I reach forward and move some hair from her face. She may be my older sister, but sometimes I feel like I need to take care of her.

Despite her having her own place to live and be, I can't blame her for not wanting to deal with the nightmares alone. I just wish she'd get help, that she'd talk to our siblings and let us find some way to assist her, to make her demons go away.

With one final pat on her hip, I stand and stretch. Before I get back to my room, I head to the kitchen to grab some water.

My house is a modest ranch with three bedrooms and two bathrooms. It's more than I need but something I can afford. Partially from my inheritance and from what I make owning the café.

When we first bought the café, we decided to put our interests and talents to work. Mazie runs the books, Alina does all the cooking, and somehow, because I love and drink the most coffee, I ended up becoming the barista.

Mazie and I have had a few conversations about my disposition and attitude toward the customers, because I'm not a bright, sunshiny person. I'm not overly friendly or sugary sweet. Having to pretend to be that way all day is utterly exhausting, and I can't stomach it most of the time.

People like Suit are part of the reason. I hate the snotty, think they're better than a small towner, assholes who come in. While we don't have too many regulars or townies like that, we do get a lot of tourists. After a few years of people watching and experience running the front end, I can tell who a more difficult customer will be. Every so often, I'm surprised, but not frequently.

The second Suit walked in, I knew.

And why would I want to know his name? So I could stop calling him Suit, maybe. But why does he care? Maybe he wants a certain level of familiarity between us.

I know his drink order, and that's really all I need to know about him. The way he looks, especially *in* his precious suits, is far more than I have any need to know. And unfortunately, I can't stop thinking about it.

He's the last kind of guy I want taking up space in my mind. Rich assholes are not my breed of man and somebody I try to stay away from.

Setting the glass in the sink, I glance at the clock. It's two in the morning, which means I'm going to be exhausted tomorrow.

Running my fingers through my curls, I head back to bed.

I need my sleep to be somewhat well rested to mentally prepare for Suit tomorrow.

Chapter 6
Jameson

It's been two weeks since I first got here. Two weeks of sleeping in a dank motel room, straining over piles of papers for hours on end, and stopping by Three Sticks at least once daily.

I still have no idea what baby Baker's name is. And she insists on calling me "Suit" instead of learning my actual name. I tried to tell her once, but she stopped me, told me again that she doesn't care, and she knows my drink order, and that's enough. If that's how she wants to play this, then game on.

Part of me has considered ordering something different to throw her off or make her reconsider knowing my name, but it's not worth it. The espresso macchiato she makes is stellar. Though I'm sort of convinced anything would be at this point.

Since I end up going around the same time of day, she's started to anticipate my arrival. Sometimes I even get a smile.

Today is one of those days. When I walk in, she grins up at me. I can tell it's mostly fake, but I like to think some of it is real.

"Afternoon, Suit. Want your usual?"

"Sure thing, Sweetheart."

"Sweetheart?" She whirls around from grabbing a cup and looks at the ceiling with the corners of her mouth turned down. "Hm. That's new."

"Well, since you won't tell me your name, I don't know what else to call you."

A wicked smile spans her face, and I know what's coming before she even speaks. "I guess *Sweetheart* it is then."

"Why won't you tell me your name?"

"Why do you need to know?"

"So I have something to refer to you as."

"I thought we just established my new nickname."

I growl and grit my teeth. She makes things extremely difficult. "Fine. *Sweetheart*. Can I also have a muffin today?"

"Any particular kind?"

"Your choice." Let's see what she does when given free rein. Will she be nice?

She hands me my coffee before brushing off her hands and bending in front of the pastry case. "Hmm." Her fingers waggle in the air as she glances up at me, then back at the case, and up at me again, before she picks one.

"Here. Mixed berry. It's one of my favorites. And they're super delicious."

One of her favorites, huh? I wonder why she's sharing both the muffin with me and that bit of information.

"So, you'll tell me your favorite muffin, but not your name?"

"Of course. It's not nearly as personal. Once you know my name, you can know so much more about me. Things I may not want you knowing." She crosses her arms over her chest, her bottom lip pouting.

A heavy sigh pulls from my chest. "You're kind of infuriating. Do you know that?"

"I have three older siblings. I've been told a time or two."

I huff and walk over to one of the several empty tables, setting down my muffin and coffee, opening my suit jacket, and sitting. Waving a hand at the empty chair across from me, I make eye contact. "Come sit with me."

Her eyes widen, and she straightens from her position. "Me?"

"No, the imaginary dragon on your shoulder. Yes, you, Sweetheart."

Though she hesitates for a minute, she eventually brushes her clothes, runs a hand through her luscious curls, and rounds the counter to come toward me. Once she sits, I'm completely taken aback by her beauty.

Her eyes are almost violet, they're so blue, and the pink compliments her dark brown curls so beautifully. She's clearly a bit more on the wild side with hair like that. Today she's wearing ripped jeans and a cut up Nirvana t-shirt that's hung over her shoulder. She's stunning.

"What are you looking at?" She leans back, giving me an unsure look.

"Nothing. Just...your wardrobe for work is highly unprofessional." I take a sip of my coffee to hide the fact that I was just ogling her. She's too young for me; I can't go there.

She lifts her bare shoulder and reaches across the table to take a piece of my untouched muffin. Popping the piece into her mouth, she rests her arms on the table in front of her. "I own the place. Or a part of it, at least. Who's going to fire me?"

"Your co-owners? They don't care what their front of house looks like?"

"I wouldn't say that, but they know it's an argument not worth having. This town has known me since I was born, and the visitors, well...let's just say, nobody has complained."

"Yet."

"Sure, yet. But if they do, what's going to change? Besides, when I'm not here, the other employees wear *appropriate* clothing." She uses finger quotes for the word "appropriate." Like our definitions are very different.

Just another sign of her infantilism.

I open my mouth to speak, but she beats me to the punch.

"Where do you live?" She reaches forward and takes another piece of my muffin, causing me to tip my head to the side.

"The city. Uh, Manhattan." I realize saying 'the city' isn't necessarily specific enough in a small town.

Her eyes widen and a twinkle skitters through them. "I've always wanted to go to the city."

"Really? A small-town girl like you?"

"Just 'cause I live here doesn't mean I *want* to be here." The way she shifts in her seat tells me there's more to things than just not getting the chance.

"Well, you're young. There's still time."

"I'm older than I seem, if only 'cause life made me that way."

An uncomfortable silence surrounds us. I'm not sure what to say because of what little I've gathered about the family. Nobody talks about them except to praise the four kids and how far they've come because of what they've been through. But what that is, nobody says.

Surely it was something heavy. Possibly tragic. But not a single person will talk about it. All it does is add to the air of mystery surrounding them and make her that much more intriguing.

While I try to think of something to say, she picks at her black nails, clearly stuck in her head. When she gets up quickly, I nearly fall out of my chair.

"Where are you going? We're having a conversation."

"First of all, we're sitting in silence. Second of all, I'm getting myself a coffee."

Leaning back slightly, I watch her as she works, smooth and comfortable in her movements around the café to make herself something. She knows what she's doing, that's for sure.

When she comes back to the table, she sets her cup down and wraps both hands around it. I've barely touched my muffin, partially so if she wants more, she can take it.

"Do you drink a lot of coffee? I mean, you work around it all day."

"More than any one person probably should." With a small nod, she lifts her cup to her perfect lips and takes a sip.

"Interesting. I never see you drinking any." I've paid attention. And not once have I seen her with a cup even near her.

"Because you come at my crazy hour, first thing in the morning when you're lucky I even acknowledge you, and now, when things are dead but I haven't yet made myself something. I'm usually still settling my lunch coffee."

"What time do you take a lunch?" Something in me needs to know.

She raises an eyebrow and I'm sure she won't answer. "Usually around one, after the rush."

"Ah, so I'm about an hour late." It makes me want to adjust my schedule and come earlier. Maybe I'll have to try that.

"Afraid so." What I can only consider to be a coy look crosses her face. Almost like she's daring me to make a move.

And I do. But not the one I think she's expecting. I wrap my muffin in a napkin and stand, buttoning my coat. "Well, it was nice chatting with you, Sweetheart. Thanks again." I lift my coffee and leave the café.

It's not until I'm on the street that I look back in to see her shaking her head with a smile on her face. The corners of my mouth perk up and my heart flutters. She seems as pleased as I am.

Chapter 7
Liv

Staring off into space isn't something I do often, but it's becoming more and more frequent lately.

My strange sit-down with Suit was three days ago, and I still don't know what to make of it.

I kept pulling pieces from his muffin because I wanted him to know that his expensive, fancy air doesn't intimidate me. But he didn't seem bothered by the fact that I was just helping myself. In fact, he didn't even eat it while he was in my vicinity. Almost like he was leaving it for me to pick at.

I'm not sure how I feel about the nickname *"sweetheart."* It's not bothering me enough that I'm going to tell him my real name, though.

"Sibby." Alina bumps my hip with hers, pulling me from my thoughts. "Again? Where is your mind lately?"

"Somewhere it shouldn't be." I start wiping down the counter once more, this time with purpose, moving on to the tables before doing the same spot over. It's what I'd been doing for the past twenty minutes or so.

"Is that somewhere tall, dark, and handsome perhaps?" She wiggles her eyebrows at me like it's not an insane thought for me to be so distracted by Suit.

"It can't be, Leen. He's not my type." With my hands held up, I shift to the next table.

"What, sexy? 'Cause he sure as hell is." She leans her forearms on the counter, linking her fingers in front of her.

"You know it's not that simple, Leen. I don't go for guys like that. And while a quick hookup would surely be fun, it can't be with him. He's too arrogant for me." My focus is on my task of cleaning the café, since this time of day is exceptionally slow for us.

"Is he? Or are you portraying him as such. The few interactions I've seen or overheard, he seems nice enough." Sometimes I hate that she reads me so well, because he has been pleasant, aside from that first time.

"He drives a Corvette, for fuck's sake." It's a sexy as hell car, but it's flashy, which isn't me.

"So? It's just a car."

"A flashy one. And those suits..." I have to swallow a groan at imagining him in one. He always looks too damn good.

"He wants to look professional at what he does. That's not a bad thing." Her gaze trails down my body, as though she's pointing out my choice in clothing.

"I own part of the business, Alina. I'm going to dress how I want to." My fists plant on my hips as I jut one out.

"And that's fine, but don't give him a hard time because he *wants* to wear a suit. It doesn't define him, Liv."

"It kind of does."

"So what? Even if it does, maybe there's more worth knowing underneath the suit."

"Alina!" Shock coils up my spine. I'm usually the forward and more sexually-minded one.

She holds her hands up in peace. "I meant mentally and emotionally. Though physically does seem like it'd be fun too."

"Mmm. That it does." I've spent far too much time thinking about what he'd be like in bed. I can't say the thoughts have disappointed me.

It takes a second for me to realize I'm drooling.

With a shake of my head and a heavy sigh, I wipe my mouth. "I just think it's best to keep it professional, Leen. Let him be a customer."

"Oh, well, speaking of, here he comes." She jerks her chin toward the door, and my eyes widen.

Immediately, my hands move to flatten my clothes and run down my hair. Alina giggles behind me, and I shoot her a look as I come around the counter, ready to greet Suit.

"Told you I'd be here a lot."

"And I'm ready for you. I'll get your drink."

"Hi. I'm Alina. I'm one of the owners and the baker."

"Ah, so you're the baker. I must give my compliments to the chef. Your muffins are delicious."

I roll my eyes as she holds a hand against her chest. "Compliments will get you everywhere."

Irritation bubbles below my skin at the way Alina is practically throwing herself at him. I don't know why my body is responding like he's mine, especially since I just made a clear argument about how I don't want him to be.

"Here's your coffee, Suit."

"Thanks, Sweetheart. Sadly, I can't stay and chat today, too busy with Seth. Just needed my caffeine jolt to get me through and let Seth take a quick break before his brain melts from all the numbers."

"Treat him right."

"I am." The sincerity in his tone and look in his eyes tell me he is. For some reason, I believe him.

With a quick nod and a lift of his coffee, he heads out, not even staying to banter a little.

"Oh man, Sibby. You got it bad."

My spine straightens and my shoulders push back. "I don't know what you're talking about."

"You should go out tonight. Call Kylee, see if she'll go with you to the club or something. It's half-price drink night."

"I don't know, Leen. It just doesn't sound as fun today."

Before I can protest, she pulls my phone from the spot where I keep it near the counter and shoots off a quick text, likely to Kylee.

I don't even try to get it back from her because it's pointless. She'll get the message out one way or another.

The responding ping comes quickly, and Alina's eyes scan the phone. "Okay, she's in. Says she'll pick you up at seven."

I huff but then think about going out with Kye. Aside from my sister, she's my best friend. It will be fun. I'd invite Alina along if I didn't know she was so exhausted from not sleeping. I'm sure she'll be asleep on the couch before I even leave for the night.

"You're right. It will be fun."

And I'm going to be sure to make it that way and forget all about Suit in the process.

Chapter 8
Jameson

"You work too much. Has anybody ever told you that?"

"All the time," I mumble without taking my eyes off the papers in my hands. "Don't feel like you have to stay." I lift my gaze to look over the tops of the sheets.

"No, you stay, I stay." He settles back into his chair and puts his hands behind his head.

"Seth, this"—I hold up the forms in my hands—"is my life. You have one outside of this office. A wife, kids. Go home, go see them, if it's not already too late." It occurs to me that it's been dark for at least an hour and everybody else left several hours ago.

"This is my livelihood. Without it, that family has nothing."

Sighing, I put down the papers. "Tell ya what, I'll go out and have some fun tonight if you go home to that wife of yours. She's going to start taking it out on me, and we don't want that."

"I can agree to that."

"So, what is there for somebody like me to do around here? Pretty sure most places have already closed. And please don't suggest any sort of festival." There was some insipid thing last weekend that I chose to check out, despite already knowing it wouldn't be for me. And I wish I hadn't. Fair food, games, prizes, and everything much too loud is not my idea of a good time.

Seth chuckles and clasps his hands together. "No festivals this weekend. Most of the kids your age head into the city and go to the bars. It's a big club night. They do half-price drinks the first Saturday of the month."

"Good business model, I suppose. Though, clubbing isn't really my thing."

"Oh, come on, Jameson. You're a young man. Go have some fun like kids your age do."

"I'm thirty, Seth. I'm well beyond my clubbing years." Way, way beyond my clubbing years. In fact, I'm not sure I've ever really been, aside from a time or two in college.

"And I'm over fifty, but I'd still go do it if the missus was interested. Get out and do something while you're still young. Besides, lots of women, from what I'm told." He raises his eyebrows like it might entice me.

The motel room is downright boring, and I haven't had any action in a while. Plus, maybe putting somebody else below me, or in front of me, will help get baby Baker off my mind.

"Alright, alright, you twisted my leg."

With one last glance at everything, I organize the paperwork how I'll want to resume looking over it tomorrow and follow Seth out.

He gets into his beat-up Honda while I hop into my Corvette. It may be flashy, but I love this damn car.

After a quick change from my suit, which doesn't seem appropriate for a club, I make the half-hour drive out toward Pineville City.

The club is bumping, literally, the floor practically shaking. I regretted coming here before I stepped in the door. It's no better once I walk through, not even once I have a drink in my hand, a whisky with far too much ice, especially since I asked for it neat.

Leaning against the bar, taking in the scene around me, I freeze, glass halfway to my lips.

She's here. Her hot pink hair flies around her as she dances. It's what catches my eye.

And fuck if she isn't sinfully sexy. I'm not sure I've ever seen her in anything besides ripped jeans, and tonight is no different, but instead of a loose, albeit low-cut, t-shirt, tonight she's paired her threads with a skintight, tank top that shows off every luscious curve of her body.

As though she can sense me, feel my eyes on her, hear my filthy thoughts, her head snaps up and our eyes meet. The air between us practically crackles. There's so much electricity, I can feel it humming along my skin.

I don't have much in the way of party clothes, seeing as I usually only hit up a bar, but I tossed on a pair of jeans and a button-down, sans the tie, cuffing the sleeves to my elbows. Taking me in, a twinkle skitters across her eyes and her tongue darts out to wet her lips.

Downing my drink, I grimace as it burns on the way down. Depending on how this interaction goes it may not be the only thing that burns.

Approaching her, I watch intently as she separates herself from the group she's with, taking a few steps back and standing straighter, chin raised high, ready to battle.

"Sweetheart."

"Suit."

"Ah, not in a suit tonight." I wave my hand down my body, as though I'm showing off a prize on a game show.

"Didn't leave it all behind, though." She plucks the material at my chest. "Plus, once a suit, always a suit. It's in your blood. Which I'm sure runs blue."

"And why is that, Sweetheart?"

"You're all about money. You wear your expensive suits every single day. I see you at least six days a week and have never seen you in anything besides dress pants. At least half the time you're in your sports coat, in the middle of the day. Not to mention that Corvette you drive around in."

So, she's noticed the car. Though by the tone, she doesn't sound overly impressed by it. "It's called working and professional attire. You may want to look into it someday."

Somebody walks past her, gently bumping into her, which causes her to stumble in my direction. Standing mere inches from each other, we're both at a loss for words.

"My attire for work is just fine. I've never gotten a single complaint." She lifts one shoulder and starts swaying her hips. It's mesmerizing.

"Yeah, I'm sure you haven't when you've got your full rack on display every single day."

Her lips curl up at the corners. "Jealous?"

"Of what? You bend over for me plenty." Instead of balking like I would expect, her eyebrow quirks in challenge.

"Of all the other patrons who get to see what you so clearly want all for yourself." Unless I'm imagining things, she definitely took a step closer. "You could dance, ya know. I mean, you are at a club."

Shifting from one foot to the other, my eyes narrow on hers. "What I want for myself? You must have a few wires crossed up there if that's what you think." I poke my finger against her temple, which she quickly bats away.

Instead of letting that be it, I grab her wrist and tug her against me. Her eyes widen and her mouth parts, but her body relaxes into mine. Hm, interesting.

Sliding my other hand down her spine, I rest it against her lower back, just above her ass, and start swaying our hips.

Responding and getting some life back in her, she wraps her hand around my neck and presses her pelvis against mine. When she starts to move her face closer, for a second I wonder if she's going to kiss me, but she turns to the side.

"Liv." The word vibrates against my chest.

"Huh?"

"Liv. My name. It's Liv."

When she lowers to flat feet, her bottom lip is caught between her teeth. Liv. That's the name of this little firecracker who I can't get out of my head, no matter how hard I try.

"Jameson. Nice to know your name, Sweetheart."

"You too, Suit."

She spins away from me, and I'm worried she's leaving, but instead she presses her back to my chest and slides herself down my body and back up before moving her ass right against my dick. Which responds immediately.

I slip one hand into her front pocket and tug in her flush against me. The other, I slide up her front, curling my fingers around her neck and tipping her head back against my chest. I feel her breath catch and hear a faint moan leave her pretty lips.

When she tilts her face toward mine, I can't help myself any longer and give in to the urge I've had for weeks.

Crashing my mouth to hers, every single molecule in my body ignites. She turns in my hold, parting her mouth as my tongue dives in, slipping along hers. My hands slide down to her thighs, and I lift her without hesitation, needing more of her. Liv wraps her arms around my neck, her legs around my waist, and I lose a hand in her mess of curls.

Our kiss is wild, heated. She tugs at my hair and bites at my lips while I squeeze her ass and yank her head backwards to lick along the curve of her neck.

"Take me back to your place." The words rush out faster than I can stop them.

"No, take me to yours."

"My shitty motel room on route four?"

"Yeah, you're right. My place."

Before I can set her down, she collides her mouth with mine, tightening her legs around my waist and squirming against me. My dick hardens beneath her, and I can't remember the last time, if ever, that I was this turned on by a kiss.

"I need to get you home. Now."

She smiles in response, and it's just about the best thing I've ever seen.

Lowering herself, she holds up one finger and stands on her tiptoes to look around. Her eyes alight when she finds who she's looking for and she takes off, me following on her tail to make sure this isn't some ruse she's established.

She grabs a redhead by the bicep and talks into her ear, hiking a thumb over her shoulder, which causes the redhead to glance my way. My response is a slight wave.

As soon as Liv's done with the short conversation, she takes two big steps in my direction and grabs my hand, dragging me off the dance floor.

The night air is crisp and feels delightful compared to the heat of the club, but I notice a shiver wracks through Liv. I throw my arm over her shoulder and tug her into my body.

"Where's your car? Please tell me you drove because I didn't."

"Of course I did. Have you seen my car?"

She shakes her head as we walk up to the blue sports car. I hold the door open for her, gesturing for her to sit. "Hop in."

With a hesitant look, she lowers herself into my car.

Chapter 9
Liv

The thud of the lock matches the one in my chest. Of all people, I never expected to be bringing Suit...*Jameson* back to my house. Sure, he's by far the sexiest man to ever step foot in the café, but he is absolutely not my type. One night won't hurt, though, right? I can still make his coffee without thinking about him and all the things we're about to do.

Who am I kidding? Barely a day goes by that his silver eyes don't cross my mind. After I let this happen, there will be no forgetting about him. He's here temporarily, then he goes back to wherever he's from, leaving this tiny town behind. I envy him for that.

"You going to actually open the door?" Jameson speaks low and right against my ear. A shiver races down my spine, along with his finger, almost like he's chasing the invisible sensation.

One part of me wants to ask what this is, what happens after tonight. But most of me, the part that usually wins out, doesn't care.

Swinging open the door, I take his hand and pull him into the small entryway. I toss my purse and keys down on the table, kicking off my heels and padding down the hall into the kitchen. Moments like this, I'm glad I keep the glasses higher up. Pushing up on my toes and reaching up makes my ass stick out just the right amount.

Pressing his chest to my back, Jameson appears right behind me, sliding a hand along my exposed stomach, his pinky dipping under the waistband of my jeans. "Let me help you get that." The raw huskiness of his voice mixed with the swirling scent of sage is a heady combination, and my panties nearly melt to the floor.

I spin around, and he stares down at me. I'd never paid much mind to his height before, but right now, with his hand on the shelf of the cabinet above my head, he towers over me. Not just that, but he surrounds me.

And I like it.

When he closes his mouth over mine, I forget all about the glass, all about the water I no longer need. The only thing I'm parched for now is Jameson.

Slipping my hands under the hem of his shirt, I glide them over the ridges of his abs.

He closes his hands around my hips, and while I expect him to pull me up and into his body, instead he places me on the edge of the counter. Stepping between my legs, he twists his fingers into my hair, pulling back so my head tilts up. Laying a trail of kisses along my collarbone and up my neck, he draws a moan from deep within my chest.

"Fuck, Liv. You've been stuck in my head for days. Since the first time I saw you."

Wait, what?

Before I can ask any sort of clarifying question, he grips my thighs and yanks me to the very edge of the counter, so my ass is just barely on the lip, and presses himself right against me.

"Do you feel what you do to me, Liv?" It'd be impossible not to notice his erection.

"Yes." I wiggle against it, causing him to groan and tip his head back.

His hands glide up my thighs, thumbs running along the seams, straight to my pussy, pressing firmly against my clit. They keep going, right to the button, which he quickly flicks open before pulling me against him and lowering me to my feet.

Kissing down my body, he pushes my pants down, lifting one foot at a time to carefully remove them. As though entranced by my skin, he runs his palms back up my legs, gaze following intently, before hooking his fingers in the band of my thong and pulling it off.

This time, he licks up my leg, from my ankle all the way to my pussy, where he starts laying more lavish kisses. He gently pushes against my legs so I'll part them, which I do in an instant, and runs a finger along my warm, wet, center.

"Fuck, Liv. So wet already," he murmurs right against the scorching skin of my inner thigh.

The second his tongue touches me, I have to grasp the counter for support, the air sticking in my lungs. "Holy fucking fuck."

A gentle 'hm' vibrates his lips, which only adds to the sensation.

He takes one leg and loops it over his shoulder, exposing me even more to him and his amazing tongue, which keeps licking thick stripes up my pussy. Every so often, he'll dip inside, which elicits increasingly louder moans from me.

But it's not until he starts lavishing my clit that my arms go weak and my elbows on the counter are all that's keeping me up.

He must sense this, because his hands wrap tightly around my hips and hold me against the cabinet as his tongue picks up in both speed and pressure, swirling around my clit.

"Oh, God, Jameson." If I could reach without collapsing on top of him, I'd twist my fingers into his hair.

That's when he pushes two fingers inside me. I arch back, my shoulders hitting the counter as I gasp and whimper. When I start to writhe against his mouth, he pulls my legs up so my back is flat on the granite and his face is flush between my thighs.

At no point does he stop, slow, or lose momentum, continuing to lick and suck and finger fuck me. It's incredible, and I start to tremble from the sensation.

I push up on my elbows to get a look at the dark head of hair between my thighs and practically lose myself right then and there. Never has a man looked so sexy going down on me.

But something about Jameson is different in so many ways.

He wraps his lips around my clit and sucks hard, and that's when I lose all composure, my head dropping down against the delightfully cool granite, every limb trembling and shaking, my thighs squeezing his head as I come.

Leaving me laying and supporting my weight, he kisses along the insides of my legs as I catch my breath and flutter back down to earth.

One arm moves under my back as he lifts me to sit on the edge of the counter again. Sliding his hands under the hem of my shirt, he yanks it from my body. When he leans forward and pulls my pert nipple into his mouth, my arms wrap around his head and hold him against me. I already need more.

When I pant out that request, he quickly frees himself from his jeans. Immediately, I reach down and wrap my hand around his cock, giving him a few rough strokes that cause his head to tip back with a groan and his hands to tighten on my hips.

But it's short-lived before he pushes my hands away.

Lifting me off the counter, I wrap my arms around his shoulders as he kicks out of his pants and strides down the hall. He surely has no clue where he's going, so when we get to my room, I tug at his shirt.

"This one."

Once we're inside, he lays me down on the bed and is over me not a second later.

The very moment Jameson pushes into me, everything ceases and the whole world tilts. I feel more full and complete than I ever have, and not just between my legs. Meeting Jameson's eyes, I know he feels it too.

A wholeness.

Repeatedly, he looks at the place our bodies are joined, then back at my face, his mouth slightly agape and eyes wide.

Twisting my fingers into his shirt, I tug him toward me, our mouths crashing together. Jameson supports himself, hovering above me for an extra beat before he lowers himself and sinks deeper into me.

Tearing my mouth from his, my head tips back. "Fuck."

Burying his face in the crook of my neck, he runs his tongue along my tingling skin and starts moving his hips. A few thrusts in and he groans against my shoulder. "Fuck, Liv. You feel Goddamn incredible."

All I can do is nod, as I've lost all ability to think or speak or even breathe.

Lowering onto his forearms, Jameson brushes his knuckles down my cheek. "Hey. Are you okay?"

"Mhm. Yeah, I'm fantastic, actually."

His lips tic up in a half smirk. "Yeah?"

"Oh, very much so."

With a slight tip of his hips, he pushes harder, thrusting powerfully, and a moan tears from my lips.

A growl starts in his chest and rumbles onto my skin. "This is going to be fun."

Shivers roll through my body, causing me to tremble. I have a feeling that with Jameson, that comment could mean many different things.

Dipping his head, he licks up my neck and pulls my earlobe between his teeth.

Pushing up, he moves off of me and pulls out, despite my trying to keep hold of his shirt and the vocal complaint I make at his absence. As he slides off the bed, my brows pull together, wondering what exactly he's doing.

Standing with pure fire glinting in his eyes as he looks down at me, he unbuttons his shirt, tearing it from his body and dropping it the floor.

Somehow in the hustle, I forgot that I'm the only one who ended up naked. Leaning up on my elbows, I take a minute to drink Jameson in, my mouth watering as I track the well-defined six-pack and deep V. Hot fuck, he's absolutely delicious.

Crawling back over me, he rests on his forearms, and I slide my hands up and down his chest, wrapping around his shoulders. His skin feels so good, the ripples of his muscles are incredible, and I know that tonight won't be enough to satisfy my craving.

He eases himself back into me but takes my hands and holds them in one of his above my head. My neck arches at the slight burn of stretching to accommodate him, and I couldn't hold back my moan if I tried.

"Fuck, Jameson."

"Likewise, Liv." Hearing my name from his mouth does something to me. It's different and so right in so many ways.

Once he's all the way inside me, he pauses and looks over my face. Somehow, I know he's making sure I'm ready for whatever's about to happen, so I nod. Slowly, he pulls out before slamming all the way back in. Then he does it again, and again, and again.

My body shifts higher up the bed with every thrust.

But it doesn't last long before he's pistoning into me, pressing my hands into the mattress. Taking one of my legs, he loops it around his hips, running his palm down to hold my ankle against his lower back.

He changes momentum again, now giving quick, hard thrusts while I'm splayed open for him.

My head tips back with a loud moan, and I tighten around him as I tremble. "Yes, Jameson." I wish I could scratch my nails down his back, grip his biceps, something. But instead, I'm left to grip him with my pussy, which I do, holding on longer while he continues to drive my senses crazy.

He only gets in a few more thrusts in before his head drops to my shoulder and he groans, pulsating inside me while he comes.

His tongue pokes out and runs along my collarbone before he releases my hands, which immediately hook to his shoulders and hold him to me.

Moving his body up, he connects our mouths, his tongue pushing between my lips to caress my own before he rolls to his back.

That was some of the best sex I've ever had. And now I know for certain, it can't be a one-night thing and I can't simply go back to making his coffee.

What have I done?

Chapter 10

Jameson

Air is hard to come by as my chest heaves. Turning my head slightly, I glance over at Liv and see she's struggling just as much.

"That was incredible. And I've had a lot of sex."

Groaning, I run a hand down my face. "Why would you tell me that? No guy wants to hear that the girl he just fucked has had lots of sex." Shaking my head, I stare at the ceiling and try to calm my thudding heart. "Is this a thing you do? Make eyes at some guy at the bar or club, bring him home, fuck him, and send him on his merry way?"

Turning to look at her, I'm met with fiery eyes and a straight mouth. "Is that seriously what you think of me?"

"I don't know what to think, Liv. We don't exactly know each other that well."

"Except that hasn't stopped you from thinking about me for weeks."

Groaning again, I throw my arm over my eyes. "You're not going to let me live that down. Are you?"

Chancing another look at her, she pokes her tongue through her teeth with a wicked grin pulling up the corners of her lips as she wiggles her body.

"Fantastic." Sighing heavily, I keep my gaze trained on the ceiling and swallow a heavy lump. "So, what is your number? Actually, you know what? I don't really want to know."

As she rolls onto my chest, Liv crosses her arms and rests her chin on her hands, her violet eyes meeting mine. Almost instinctively, my fingers start to trail down her spine.

"It's not really that many."

Cocking an eyebrow, I'm not sure I believe her. She's absolutely stunning, for one, and her confidence shines through. I haven't learned yet if it's surface level or deep seated, but either way, it's noticeable. And incredibly sexy.

"It's not, Jameson. Besides, I'm sure you've slept with your fair share of women. Traveling for work? No strings attached? You definitely seem like that type of guy."

"I feel like I should be offended right now." She has me pegged, but I'm not sure it's a good thing or bad thing. Maybe she's just good at reading people.

"All I'm trying to say is that I understand you have a history."

"But I didn't throw it in your face."

A genuine smile graces her face and my stomach flips at the sight. "I'm sorry. I didn't mean it that way. All I meant was that it was far superior to anything I've ever experienced before. But if I'd only had sex twice, that doesn't hold as much water. You know what I mean?"

"I guess. There are just other ways to mention it."

Rolling her eyes, she parts her arms to lay a kiss on my chest. "Noted."

We lie in silence for a moment, neither of us really sure what to say. Should I be getting up and getting dressed? Does she not know how to ask, and most other guys offer?

Clearing my throat, I move my arms from around her and shift to get up. "Well, um, I guess I better get going—" I freeze when I take in her wide eyes and parted lips. "Unless…you don't want me to?"

"Uh, I guess I kind of figured maybe we could talk? Get to know each other?" She puts her head back on my chest, facedown, and shakes it from side to side. Getting a glance at the back of her head, I notice that her curls are starting to knot together. "Sorry, that sounds ridiculous. You can leave if you want to."

When she goes to move off of me, I tighten my grip around her, causing her to look up at me. Her violet eyes steal my breath. "It doesn't, Liv. I don't want to go. I just thought you didn't want me to stay."

Not really sure where to start, we both stare at each other for another minute. As awkward at this moment may be, lying naked after a solid fucking with the woman I haven't stopped thinking about, yet know very little about, there's an undeniable connection. Some sort of chemistry, a pull, exists between us. It's palpable.

"This is silly. We're lying here naked. And we talk every single day." Thankfully, she breaks the silence with what I was already thinking.

"Agreed."

Adjusting herself with a shimmy of her whole body, she shakes her head and dives in. "Okay, so we already know I'm twenty-three. And you are…"

"Thirty."

"Alright, not too terrible." Did she think I was older? Younger?

"When's your birthday? Mine's in October."

"May."

"So from October to May, I'm actually eight years older than you."
I'm not sure I'm on the same page with her about the age gap.

"I guess so. Does it really matter, though?"

"I mean, you are practically a baby. You've only been able to drink for, like, two years."

"Legally." My mouth pulls down at the corner with her need to point that out. It's the childish aspect of her.

"Doesn't matter."

"Is it some sort of deal breaker for you?" She stiffens.

"Are we making some sort of deal?"

She lifts one shoulder, glancing down at my chest as she swirls a fingertip along my collarbone. "I don't know. Maybe. I could be reading things wrong, though."

"Why pink?" Taking a lock of the pink her hair, I twirl it around my finger, changing the subject. It's soft and vibrant. The very opposite of any girl I've ever held an interest in before. And yet...

"Why not? I don't know...there's a lot of things in my life I don't have control over, a lot of things I do because I have to or feel an obligation to do. But my hair? I do have control. I can do what I want, how I want, when I want."

"And your business attire? Do you have the same mentality for that?"

"There's nothing wrong with my business attire, Jameson." I can see the irritation in her eyes. I should probably drop it.

"Except that it's not *business*."

"It's comfortable and casual. Like us, like our shop. Nobody has to wear a uniform, nobody has to feel like we have expectations. Don't dress like a whore at work and you're fine."

Raising an eyebrow, I stay silent until she looks at me.

"Oh please, I am *not* dressing like a whore. My shirts may be a touch revealing if I bend a certain way, but I know exactly what I'm doing."

"And the way your ass sticks out when you reach for something?" A twinge settles in my dick as it starts to harden. Just thinking about her perfect body makes it difficult to do anything else.

Not realizing her movement, I gasp when her fingers wrap around my quickly growing erection. "Fuck, Liv."

"Yeah, I'd like to. Again." Throwing her leg over my hip, my hands slide down her back to grab her perky ass.

Leaning forward, she closes her mouth over mine. When she starts to lean back, I cup the back of her neck, keeping her against me, sliding my tongue along the seam of her lips so they part. Slipping my other hand between our bodies, I run my fingers along her soaking cunt and dip two inside.

The moan starts in her throat, and I swallow it down. Hooking my fingers inside her, I let her tear her mouth from mine and throw her head back. She's so damn gorgeous.

When her brow creases and she starts grinding against my hand, I can't take it anymore and replace my fingers with my cock. I'm certain I'm harder than I've ever been. Taking her hips in my hands, I ease her down slowly, watching her face change and her breaths stutter with every inch.

Once I'm all the way inside her, her hands firmly against my chest, I give the smallest tilt up of my hips. The small whine that comes from Liv is one of the sexiest sounds I've ever heard.

Gripping her waist tighter, I start pushing forward and back, every few thrusts tipping up my pelvis. Liv's eyes are shut tight, her mouth agape, and her brows knit together. Sheer pleasure consumes her, and I can't get enough of it.

Digging her nails into my chest, her head flies backward and her breasts heave. "Jameson."

Nobody has ever said my name that way. Like it's the only name that could ever possibly be uttered by her impeccable mouth.

It snaps the last ounce of restraint I have in me.

Wrapping my arms around her and cupping her head, I flip us so she's flat on her back. Her eyes fly open as she lays stunned for a moment, but it all disappears when I hook her ankle over my shoulder and plow into her relentlessly.

The arch of her back, the squirm of her tight body, and the incredible sounds she's making have me second guessing my existence and everything I've done up to this point.

The way she feels around me and looks underneath me, it's like nothing has ever been before and it's something I want to experience over and over.

It all drives me as I thrust hard and fast into her perfectly tight and wet pussy. The faster I move, the more she whimpers and the tighter her nails dig into my shoulders.

But it's not enough; it's not what I need right now. I pull out, gripping her hips and flipping her onto her stomach. Grabbing a pillow from the top of the bed, I bunch it up tight and put it under her stomach so her ass is raised a little bit but not all the way.

Then I dive back into her in one full thrust. The moan that tears from her mouth is the most delicious sound I've ever heard.

I pull out slowly before slamming back in, her hair splayed all around her in a brown and pink halo, a smile gracing her face. I repeat the motions a few times before my need gets the better of me.

Licking down her spine, I rest over her back, taking her hands in mine and linking our fingers while I fuck her into the mattress.

"Fuck, Jameson. Oh, fuck. I'm gonna come. Fuck. Don't stop." Her words drive me wild. Not just the words themselves but how they come out with a tiny whine. She's utterly breathless.

I adjust her slightly on the pillow and groan at how deep I can reach. She takes my cock so perfectly. Clamping down around me, her body trembles and her fingers grip mine tightly as she screams out her release.

There's no slowing or stopping as I continue to fuck her until I come buried deep inside her.

I drop my forehead to the crown of her head and leave a light kiss against her curls before rolling to my side and propping my head on my elbow.

"Sorry, what were we talking about?"

A smile breaks across her face as she turns to face me full on, a hand running down my arm. "My business attire."

Jealousy is a cruel mistress. I barely know this woman, but I hate to even think about the fact that if I can see her like that, so can anybody else.

But she must read my thoughts, because she crawls onto my chest and brushes her lips against mine. "Don't worry. I only show off the goods for you."

And for some reason, that takes a heaviness off my chest and adds a lightness to my body. She only shows off for me?

Some part of me had thought that maybe we'd fuck and I'd get her out of my system. After all, we're both adults.

Now I realize that I'm a damn fool.

Chapter 11
Liv

Jameson is nothing like I first expected. Yes, he wears a suit every day and is a professional, but he's not stuck up. In fact, I've found him to be very down to earth.

The Corvette is something he'd always wanted, and when he finally had the money for it, he decided to buy it. While he could afford a more expensive car, he loves it.

"So does everybody call you Jameson?" I'm sprawled across his chest while he plays with my hair and trails his fingers down my back.

"My friends call me Jay."

"Jay. Interesting. So, what should I call you?"

He tucks a curl behind my ear. "Anything you want."

"Really? Anything?" A devilish smile spreads across my lips.

"Within reason," he grumbles. I'm sure he's thinking of me calling him a douchebag when we met. "Is Liv short for anything?"

"Olivia. But nobody really calls me that."

"Not even your parents?"

I stiffen and try not to make it too obvious. I'm not ready to tell him that story.

"Nope, not even them." A lump takes root in my throat and its vines wind down around my heart.

"So how do you come to be a partial owner of a bakery at twenty-three? Even I'm impressed by that one."

"That's another story for another time."

"And Three Sticks?"

"Three of us sisters. Alina, you've met her, she does the baking and all that jazz. Mazie does the bookkeeping. You'd probably like her; she's very numbers oriented. But she does a good job, and we make a good profit."

"That's in large part to your excellent coffee, pastries, and other services." He gives my ass a firm swat.

"People don't come back to gawk, Jameson. This whole town knows me and my siblings. They have since we were young. They're not going to hit on me just because I wear a shirt that dips a little lower in the front." While I may use it to my advantage at times, I keep myself friendly and professional, regardless of what he may think. Plus, this town knows me too well. They know my life down to the very finite details, including every aspect of what happened to us years ago.

It's the outsiders, the visitors, he needs to be worried about, but I won't tell him that.

"Well, you guys seem to do well for yourselves. That's impressive at young ages."

"You talk like you're *so* much older than me. It's just a few years, Jameson. And what is that in the grand scheme of things? It's just a number, and I have far more life experience than you may think." My jaw sets tightly and there's a slight bite to my tone.

If he picks up on it, he glazes right over it. "How do you survive in this tiny town? There's nothing to do."

"We don't really know anything different. And the city isn't too far away. It's not the same as living in a big city like Manhattan, but it's got enough."

"Did you always want to stay here?"

I scoff at his suggestion. "No way. I had dreams of getting the hell out of here, but things changed and that just didn't happen." Before he has a chance to ask what exactly happened, a story I'm not ready for yet, I turn the tables to focus on him. "So, you're here helping Seth. Tell me about that."

Though I nod and do my best to listen along while he talks, there's a heaviness weighing in my chest and on my mind. We may be lying in bed naked and have fucked a handful of times, but I don't know him well enough yet for him to know me on a deeper level.

It's not a story I share with just anybody, and if I'm going to share it with him, we need to be in a relationship of some sort. And that's not something I'm sure he's looking for. Hell, I'm not sure if *I'm* looking for that with him. I certainly didn't come into this expecting anything more than a fun night, maybe two.

But now that we've been together, something shifted, and there's more here than just a crush. One that up until now I've basically refused to accept I have, except for the fact that I couldn't get him out of my head.

I thought I needed to get him in bed, that it'd soothe the itch and then it'd be gone. Instead, it's now a full-blown rash that's driving me crazy, and I need more. Right now, it feels like no amount of Jameson would be enough and not just because he fucks like a God.

No, this man has already started to dig his claws into me and I'm afraid before long, I'm going to be a goner. For a man who's set to leave.

This has no way to end but in tragedy. Though that'd be consistent with the story of my life.

Chapter 12

Jameson

We've been in bed for hours, bouncing between sleeping, talking, and fucking. Based on our very casual conversations, I've learned my initial thoughts about Liv were very wrong. She's far from young and dumb. Young, yes, dumb, not even a little. The way she talks and the things she says are both intelligent and wise beyond her years. It's easy to tell she's aged beyond her early twenties. There's a maturity about her that comes out in a way I haven't seen in our previous interactions.

When both our stomachs grumble at the same time, Liv lays a trail of kisses up my abs, landing on my lips, and pushing up on her elbows.

"We should eat." She says the words against my mouth, a hunger in her eyes that's not for food.

"Yeah, that's probably a good idea. We need to replenish our fuel and then some." My hands slide around her waist and hug her tightly to me.

"You should shower."

"You should join me."

"I can do that later. I'm going to cook."

Before I can answer or finish the kiss I've started to lean in for, she's out of bed and standing, stark naked and perfect, in front of her dresser. Digging through it, she tosses a pair of sweatpants and a t-shirt on the bed.

Sitting up, the sheet pooling around my hips, one leg sticking out, I eye the clothes skeptically. I'd rather my two-day old club clothes than something left over from an old boyfriend.

I glance at her just in time to catch the roll of her eyes. "They're my brother's." She's already walking away and into the bathroom.

"Wait, you have a brother?"

Glancing over her shoulder, a wicked smile stretches her lips. "Yup."

Without giving me even a modicum more, she disappears into the bathroom.

Fuck, I can deal with sisters. But brothers are a different story. They're more protective, especially of their sisters.

Falling back to the bed, I throw my arm over my eyes and groan.

"He's not so bad, Jameson. I promise." She comes back over and gives me a quick peck on the cheek, and I reach my other arm out to cup her ass, now covered in a soft fabric.

I groan inwardly at the fact that she put panties on and further refuse to uncover my eyes.

"Take a shower, wear the clothes. They're Eli's, they're clean, and you two are about the same size. You'll just have to go commando, but I'm sure you don't have a problem with that."

Before I can stop her, she slips from my grip. I can sense the moment she's out the door. The air changes pressure and sensation when she's no longer in my presence.

Flopping my hand to the bed, I stare at the ceiling for an extra minute or two. This wild, fantastic, crazy, wonderful woman has rocked my world in a matter of thirty-six hours. She'd already started to sway it, to tilt it on its axis toward her, but now, it's completely shifted.

There's been some sort of pull toward her since the moment we met, something I couldn't quite put a finger on. But now that I've felt her, touched her, tasted her, there's absolutely no going back.

And there lies the biggest problem. Even if I could get past our age gap, I'm here for work and leave in a handful of weeks. So where would that leave things?

"Fuck."

Tossing off what's left of the sheet, I take Liv's advice and opt for a shower. Like so much of her house, the bathroom is nicely appointed with an all-tile shower. I immediately note that it's more than big enough for two people and add that to the ever-growing list in my head of places to enjoy her and her body.

The list I shouldn't have.

Letting the water run down my back, I lean my forearms against the wall. This was not a position I ever thought I'd find myself in. Not only have I done far more than just a single hookup with some floozy in a random town, I've now formed a connection, which I never do because of the short-term nature of my job. It seems crazy to go from some nice banter each day for my coffee to what it feels like now.

Though, maybe that feeling is one sided. It's entirely possible that Liv does this all the time. That she meets a guy at the club or a bar, brings them home and fucks them senseless, and then sends them on their merry way. She didn't want me to leave last night, but maybe she just wanted more time.

The thought sends my stomach roiling. I have no right to feel any claim to her. In so many ways, I still barely know her. And yet, some part of me has this sense of ownership. Not in a way that I actually *own* her, but that I get her heart, her soul.

"You're a fucking idiot, Jameson Penshir."

Shutting off the water, I grab the neatly folded and fluffy blue towel that Liv clearly set out for me.

Once I'm dried and dressed, I head to the kitchen, where I find Liv standing at the stove, moving her hips back and forth to music only she can hear.

In my shirt.

My gray button-down is huge on her, the sleeves rolled up as she moves something that smells mouthwatering around in the pan. Or maybe she's what's mouthwatering. I can't quite tell as my gaze is fixated on her ass.

I can't exactly see it, with the shirt hanging just below. But every so often, she'll shift on her feet or reach to grab something, and when she does, the shirt lifts, exposing those perfectly shaped cheeks.

The feeling I had in bed increases tenfold. I could wake up to this every morning, walk in to this every night. Any time of day.

Clearing my throat before I say or do something I may regret, she turns, eyes wide for all of a second before they crinkle with her smile.

"There you are. I'm just cooking us up some food. Have a seat." She points her spatula at the barstools set against the island.

Instead of sitting, I slowly make my way toward her. "It smells incredible."

"I'm certainly not the chef of the family, but Alina taught me a few things. This is one of my favorites. Oh!" She hadn't looked at me while she responded, so when I wrap my arm around her waist and tug her to me, I catch her by surprise.

"Hi." I'm holding her so close that my lips brush against hers. Her jasmine scent wafts into my nose. She always has the slightest essence of coffee to her, which must be from working around it all day. This woman is absolutely intoxicating.

"Hi yourself." Pinching her bottom lip between her teeth, she tracks my chest as I opted to forego the shirt.

"I've had fun so far." I have to tip my head far down to look at her. There's a definite height difference here. But I love it, as I cage her in against the counter. I'm completely surrounding her.

"So have I."

"Notice I said, 'so far.'" This is a very key element. If she doesn't reciprocate my want to stay, then I'll have to find a new place to get coffee.

"I did."

"That means I'm not ready for this to be over."

"You'll hear no arguments from me." Her eyes lift to mine and they're full of need.

"We both have to work tomorrow."

She gives one solemn nod. "We do. I have to be at the café by five-thir-ty." Wow, she's an early waker.

"Do you mind if I spend the night again?" Though I'm asking, if she says no, I'm going to have to convince her.

"You better." Standing up on her toes, she links her fingers behind my neck.

"And what about tomorrow? After work?"

"I could be convinced to invite you over again. Probably tomorrow. Maybe the rest of the week." She lifts her shoulder and tries to look nonchalant, but I see through her and know that's exactly what she wants. "Who knows."

With no words to say, I crash my mouth to hers, losing a hand in her hair and cupping the back of her head. Her arms loop around my neck, and her legs circle my waist as I lift her.

Turning us around, I swipe off the counter. A cutting board and dozens of chopped vegetables go thudding to the floor. Neither one of us cares as I set her on the edge of the granite. She hisses for a second as the cold material hits bare skin, and I take the opportunity to start kissing and sucking along her throat and neck while I slide the hem of her shirt up her thighs.

"You, in my shirt, so fucking sexy."

The warm skin beneath my palms pebbles as I glide them up along her smooth, flat stomach. Keeping my mouth against her neck, her forearms rest on my shoulders and her head tips back.

Cupping her breasts, her breath catches, and her legs tighten, pulling me closer. This is the most I've ever fucked in one weekend. It's like we just can't get enough of each other, and it's certainly true for me.

I run my thumbs over her hardened nipples, causing her to whimper and tip her head back. The mixture of brown and pink curls cascade down her back in the most beautiful way.

Caressing my hands along her soft skin, I slip them from the shirt and start to slowly unbutton it, my gaze heated and fixated on only Liv. Her head snaps up and a look of irritation is planted on her face as she meets my eyes.

"Faster."

"No, no, darling. I get to decide to speed. I want to slowly undress you from the little you have on. Then I'm going to fuck you right here on this counter."

She moans and nods in agreement.

Once I've undone all the buttons, I trail my fingers along her curves, starting at her thighs and working my way up. My dick pulsates in my pants, begging to come out and play.

If I wasn't so damn hungry, I'd bury myself inside Liv right now and spend the rest of my day there, but as it is, I'm surprised I'm standing and functioning with all the energy I've burned and not replaced.

Dipping my head, I pull one of her nipples into my mouth, keeping my eyes on her face to watch as it crumples with pleasure. Her fingers dive into my hair and pull my head closer while she wiggles her ass on the counter.

I straighten and wrap my hands around her thighs, pulling her the slightest bit more off the edge before freeing my cock.

One thing I've learned so far is that she's very responsive to my touch, and always ready for me. With one final look in her eyes, I plunge deep inside her, causing her to moan and rest her forehead against my shoulder.

Her black painted fingernails dig into my skin, and she tilts her hips toward me, my sign she wants more.

Cupping her ass, I start thrusting hard and fast. I tug her toward me with each thrust in, her breasts practically in my face as she arches backward.

With a slight dip down, I pull her nipple into my mouth and lavish it with my tongue while continuing to pound into her.

Her fingers twist through the short hairs at the back of my head as she whines for more.

When I bite down, she jerks in my hold, a scream ripping from her mouth as she tightens around me and trembles.

"Oh fuck, oh fuck, oh fuck. Jameson." God, the way she says my name when she comes. Every time is slightly different, but all equally amazing.

I release her nipple with a pop and pull her from the counter, turning us around and slamming her against the fridge, magnets and pictures falling to the ground. Her legs wrap around my waist again, the heels of her feet pressing against my ass as I continue my vicious thrusts. The fridge moves with the force.

She's so slick and wet, I never want to leave her pussy. But the familiar sensation of an impending orgasm is creeping up on me.

Gripping her ass tightly, I give a few more hard pounds up into her and release, coming deep inside her.

I rest my forehead against the cool metal in front of me and breathe heavily for a moment before I grab the closest towel to clean her up with before setting her back on flat feet.

She brushes some hair from her face and rebuttons her shirt before perking up on her toes and kissing my cheek, one hand landing on my shoulder to support her. Silently, she turns back to the stove.

"Look. It's still good."

"Even if it wasn't, it'd be worth it." I step around her to the coffeepot and look around. "Mugs?"

She juts her chin toward the cabinet next to me. "Right above."

Pulling out two coffee cups for us this feels right in a strange way. Nothing about it feels new or awkward or even like I shouldn't be doing it.

The notion itself is enough to be life-altering, but somehow Liv makes me comfortable, confident, and like I can be myself around her.

I'm going to need much, much more of this girl.

Chapter 13
Liv

"You've been in a disgustingly good mood recently. Anything you want to tell me?" Kylee is sitting across from me at one of the tables for our weekly coffee date.

"You know that guy I left the club with last weekend? Well, I've been seeing him every day since then."

"Yesss! Finally." She rolls her eyes and crosses her arms against her chest.

"What do you mean, finally?"

"You needed somebody who was going to rope you in and keep you centered. You're happy. Look at you."

"That's what I keep telling her." Alina sing-songs her way over with three muffins in hand. She usually joins us. "The best part? He's a suit."

"No way. You're dating a guy who wears a suit? I never thought I'd see the day." Though the guys I pick tend to be more of a jeans and ratty t-shirt type, I'm not sure the assessment is fair.

"You guys are making a big deal out of nothing. Besides, he's here temporarily. I'm just having some routine fun while he's here."

The two of them make eye contact and shake their heads with smiles on their faces.

"What?"

"The way you talk about him, you're way more invested than just *some fun until he leaves*." Alina would point that out.

"And you're happier than I've seen you with a guy in...maybe ever."

"You two are blowing this way out of proportion. He's good in bed. It makes me happy. I'm getting laid daily. What's not to like?" I'm definitely downplaying what's going on with Jameson. I have to. They can't know I'm developing feelings with somebody I recently met and who's leaving in a few weeks.

I'd say I barely know him, but after our time together, I feel like I do. We've chatted and learned things about each other. Not necessarily anything too deep, but I know he lives in Manhattan, that he grew up an only child in Connecticut with a single mom. He seemed distracted enough about his own life that he didn't ask too much about mine, which I appreciated since I'm still not ready for that conversation.

Most importantly, he's single. He's not out here living it up, following some weird rule about being away. Apparently, the travel makes it hard to settle down, but he hasn't met the right woman yet, not that he's sure he wants to. I'm not sure how that sits with me.

It's not that I've even thought in terms of Jameson being somebody real for me. That's insane; our...whatever this is, has an expiration date. But it's just frustrating to be with a man who feels that way about this aspect of life.

A hand waves in front of my face. "Earth to Liv. Where'd you go?" Kye leans in front of me, so I lock eyes on her.

"Sorry, just thinking."

"About your new beau?"

"Maybe a little. It all has an expiration date, guys. He's leaving. So, it can be fun and games until then, but that's it." I cross my hands as I say it.

"What if he doesn't leave?" Alina tilts her head to the side, as though it's a real question.

"Of course he's going to go back to his life in the city. Why wouldn't he? I would if it were me." Alina stiffens beside me, and I let my eyes fall shut. Me staying here is a big topic of contention amongst my siblings. I feel like I need to stay, even if they've encouraged me to leave and go live my life where and how I want. But I'm stubborn and refuse.

"Leen, you know what I mean." But it's too late, and I've upset her. She thinks I only stay because of her, which isn't true.

She stands, wiping crumbs from the front of her pants. "It's time for me to get back to work anyway."

Without another word, she walks away and disappears behind the counter and into the kitchen.

"Ugh." I let my head fall to my arm on the table, thudding it lightly against the wooden surface.

"She'll get it eventually, Liv. Just give her time." Kylee understands why I stay. She knows it's more than just Alina, more than her nightmares, more than my siblings as a whole.

For one, I've built a life here. I own part of the café, have a house, a community, my best friend. There's more for me here than just my siblings.

The bell chimes, and I glance up. It's about the time that Jameson would be coming in for the day. But instead, I'm greeted by Mazie and Elijah.

A smile breaks across my face at the sight of my older siblings, who come in already chatting intently about something.

Kylee's face turns pink, and she tucks some red hair behind her ear. She's had a crush on Eli since we were kids, but he doesn't date women that much younger than him, much to her chagrin.

I stand and walk over to them, barreling right into Eli. He's the only boy with us three girls, and he takes it in stride. He's my hero.

"Hi, big bro."

He wraps his arms around me tightly and squeezes me into his side. "Babiest sis." Eli's the oldest of us all, and I'm the youngest. It gives us a special sort of bond.

We all have our unique relationships with one another, then as a core four.

Letting him go, I move to my sister. "Hey, Zee. What brings you by, today?" If she's here, it's likely only for work purposes.

"Can't I come see my baby sisters?"

I pull back and raise an eyebrow at her.

"Okay. I wanted to look over the books and talk to Alina about some new menu ideas. And I have some concerns about this new boyfriend of yours." Mazie runs the whole operation that we have here. If not for her, we likely wouldn't be as successful as we are.

"And I'm just here for the food." Eli pats his non-existent belly. How he stays fit, I have no idea. The man eats like no other.

Kylee stands and comes over to us. I almost forgot she was still here. "Liv, I'm going to go."

I separate myself from my siblings and give her a hug. "Thanks for swinging by. We'll catch up next time. Sorry, we didn't get to finish."

"I want more details next time."

Eli and Mazie make themselves comfortable behind the counter, getting coffee and taking a few pastries. Well, Eli takes a few. Mazie takes one.

"Promise." The bell chimes again as she leaves, and I turn around to watch as Alina comes out and gives our big siblings hugs.

Now comes my least favorite part of working here. Actual work.

Chapter 14
Jameson

We're at Liv's house, which has become our typical locale, her head on my chest, and her hair splayed around her. I have a curl between my fingers, twisting it repeatedly.

"You keep your hair pretty long." It's down to her mid-back dry and grazes her ass in the shower.

"That way, there's something to grab onto," she mumbles.

"What?"

"What?"

And then it dawns on me. "Liv. Do you like your hair pulled?"

Her face pinks. "Maybe."

Wrapping my hands around her biceps, I lift her and pull her toward me. "Don't be shy, Sweetheart. If you tell me what you like, I can incorporate it."

"Don't do it for my benefit. I don't like that. I want a man who takes control and does what he wants with me."

At this, I raise an eyebrow. I've been holding back a bit for her. Pull her hair? Child's play. I wonder how she'd feel about my hand wrapped around her delicate throat. Hopefully good.

She snuggles back into her spot on my chest. It appears she favors being on my right side and laying across me to rest her ear over my left pec. Her fingers dance along my exposed skin.

We have a lot of moments like this when we're just lying together, silently enjoying one another's presence. It's not an awkward silence, not something that's a result of not knowing what to say. It just is. And it's peaceful.

"Did you guys open a café because your last name is Baker?" It's a question I've asked a few times in a few different ways that I still have yet to get an answer to.

"Uh, not exactly. It's a long story...for another time." It's impossible not to notice that her demeanor completely changes. While she had been facing me, swirling her fingertip along my collarbone, now she's turned away, hand closed and her body tight.

There's something, something *big*, that's affecting this family, these *siblings*, as she'd say.

She hasn't opened up to me about it, and I won't rush it, won't push her. I know she'll share with me when she's ready. The fact that I've asked a few times is my gentle way of opening the door, letting her know I'm here.

Twisting my fingers through her hair, I pull her attention back to me.

"You can talk to me, Liv. I'm here for you, for all of it. We've been seeing each other for a few weeks. I'd like to think you know who I am by now and that I won't judge you."

"It's just not that simple. Trust me, I'll tell you if and when I'm ready." I don't love the *if and when* aspect of that sentence, but I'll take what I can get. Instead of changing subjects, I just hold her and run my fingers through her hair while I let her feel whatever emotions she needs to right now.

It's in these raw moments that I see more with her. There's an end date to this, and it's when I leave; we know this. But more and more, I'm feeling dread at that prospect. Not of leaving the small town, but of leaving its star barista behind.

I could ask her to come with me, to join me in Manhattan and travel with me and be by my side. But for some reason, I don't think she'd go for it. Her family is important to her, and while I haven't met them, I know that's artfully designed by her. She doesn't want me to know them yet, and I can't blame her when we haven't discussed what this is or where it's going.

At some point, soon, I need to find a way to tell her that I'm here, that I'm in, and that I want her. For more than just the few weeks I have left.

Chapter 15
Liv

"**M**aze. What are you doing here again? We just went over the books a few days ago. We're putting into practice what you suggested and raised the price on the few lattes. Alina came up with something seasonal, and I'm experimenting with a new drink." All the things she thought would be good ideas, we're doing.

So then why is she standing in front of me?

It's not that I don't love my sister. It's more that we have a tumultuous relationship. We always have. Probably because she needed to mommy me more than Alina, and definitely not Eli. I needed punishing and she was all too happy to dole it out. I can't even count how many times I was grounded for things like breaking curfew, going to parties, getting *caught* at parties, and having trouble at school. Which I, of course, rebelled against because Mazie was not my mother, but my sister.

"We never got a chance to talk about your new boyfriend."

I managed to get around that conversation last time. "We're not exactly the sit and gossip duo. Besides, you've never really shown interest before. Why now?"

"I've seen him around town, and I have some concerns." Of course she does. How could I not see that's where this is coming from?

Sucking my teeth, I toss the towel down on the counter and lean on my forearms. "And what exactly are your concerns, Mazie?" Fire resides in my eyes and flickers through my veins. She doesn't even know Jameson; how dare she judge him.

"Well, my biggest one is that he's here temporarily. What happens when he leaves? You're here, all caught up on some guy, who's probably married with a wi—"

"Jameson is not cheating on anybody. He's single."

"So he's told you."

"And I believe him. He's practically married to his job, Maze."

"You barely know him."

I stiffen and straighten to stand. "I'm going to stop you there. I know him more than you realize. We've been together for a few weeks now and have spent much of that time getting to know each other."

"Sure, in bed." She scoffs like that means nothing. But Mazie's never really understood the importance of intimacy, and she thinks I understand it a little too much.

"Beyond that. We know each other on a deeper level."

"That's impossible. It's been weeks. Not months."

"It is possible, Mazie, because it's how we feel. Why are you judging him when you haven't even met him? Where is this coming from?"

"I've seen him around plenty in those expensive suits, driving that Corvette around. He's not like us, Livie. He's not small-town, and he doesn't seem the type who would consider giving up city life. What are you going to do, go with him?"

"For one, I wouldn't ask him to do that. Secondly, you know I wouldn't leave you guys. I don't know why you're talking about him like he's about to propose marriage. We're having fun, and I enjoy his company."

"I'm talking like this because he's practically moved into your house, Livie. And the way you talk about him, how different you seem in recent weeks."

"But it's a good different, isn't it? So what if that's because of Jameson?"

"I'm just worried that when he leaves, you're going to fall apart."

Pulling my shoulders back, I tip my chin up. "When have you ever known me to fall apart? Especially because of a man."

"Never. But I've also never seen you like this before. Which is why I'm worried."

I take a moment to really look her over. She does look truly concerned as her eyes roam my face.

My posture slackens. "Mazie, please, get to know him. For me. I never ask you for anything. You know that. This...it's one thing I'm asking for."

Her eyes narrow as she looks me over. She must be weighing her options and wondering what my recourse would be if she said no.

"Fine. Group dinner. We'll all be there."

My eyes grow wide. "What? No. That's not fair to gang up on him like that."

"It's group dinner or nothing."

"Ugh. Fine!" I have no choice but to give in.

A victorious smile spans her face, and she taps the counter. "Good. Let's do tomorrow, my house."

"How about Alina's house as neutral territory?"

"Hmm. Deal. She'll want to cook anyway, makes it easier on her."

Any time we all have dinner, Alina insists on cooking.

"Alright. Tomorrow at Alina's. But you have to tell her."

"Not a problem. I'll go do that now."

The smile stays planted on her face as she walks behind me and into the kitchen.

My head falls to the counter, and I bang it a few times, exasperated. Now I get to tell Jameson that he's having dinner, with all of my siblings, in one night.

He's barely even met Alina.

I hope this doesn't scare him away.

Chapter 16

Jameson

"Thank you for coming with me tonight." She says it like I had any choice but to say yes. The dinner is basically being hosted in my honor.

"Of course, Sweetheart." I hold her chin and pull her lips to mine.

We're sitting in the Corvette, waiting. We've been sitting here for ten minutes, but she's not ready to go in yet. I can tell from the way she's sunken in her seat and hasn't moved a muscle.

"You good?"

She glances at the clock again. "Um. Not yet."

"Liv, I can't be late to the dinner that's basically being thrown as a way to roast me."

Her eyes are large and wide and the corners of her lips tip down. A chuckle pulls from my chest. "It's okay, baby. I know what tonight's about. I'm happy to meet your siblings. I'll take anything that comes my way."

I haven't told her yet, but I'm falling in love with her. I'm an idiot for letting it happen, but I'm pretty sure it was beyond my control. Like some greater force is at play here.

Her whole chest heaves as she sighs. "Okay. Let's go."

She's not quite ready, not making a move to get out of the car, so I straighten the cuffs on my shirt and walk around to her side, opening her door and holding out a hand while the other plants in my jeans pocket.

When I asked about the dress code, Liv had said it'd be casual, just jeans. But I didn't bring too many casual shirts. Not to mention, I want to make a good impression, so I stuck to one of my day-to-day button-downs.

Liv looks stunning in a tight black shirt and jeans. The pink in her hair pops against the darkness. As she stands in front of me, she's a picture of nervous energy.

With a light chuckle, I cup her face and run my thumbs along the apples of her cheeks.

"It's going to be okay, Liv. I can handle anything they throw my way."

Her eyes shift from the house behind me to mine. "You don't know Mazie."

"No, but I deal with difficult clients, day in and day out. I got this."

Though her mouth presses into a line, she nods and links her fingers with mine. I grab the bottle of wine from the passenger seat and shut the door, letting her lead me up to the house.

We pause at the front door, and I wonder if she's going to ring the bell, when she takes a deep breath, plasters on a smile, and lets us in.

"We're here." Her voice echoes in the small entryway, where we take our shoes off.

Before we can make our way farther into the house, the three siblings come to us.

Having all four of them together, you can definitely see the family genes. They all look very similar with darker hair, the girls all have curls, and their eyes are all the same shape.

"Welcome." Alina's half-behind the wall, her hand resting on it, and a smile on her face. But it seems like a nervous smile, not like the happy ones I've seen here and there while at the café. She doesn't come out of the back much when I'm around. I'm not sure if that's intentional or if that's her hideout.

"Thank you for inviting me. Here, I brought this for you." I hand her the bottle of wine. I wanted to get the most expensive, but Liv argued against it, saying that I don't want to be showing off that I have money.

"Oh, thank you. We can have it with dinner. It'll pair nicely with the lasagna."

Quietly, I take in the rest of the scene. Liv is pressed into her brother's side, and he has a protective arm around her, but he doesn't seem overly irritated by my presence. And then the other sister, Mazie, is glaring at me with her arms crossed. I wish I could say she was just looking at me, but there's no other way to describe it other than a glare.

"Come in, come in. Let's get out of the entryway." Alina starts to walk away, waving us into her modest house. It's not terribly dissimilar to Liv's, though it seems flipped. Where Liv's rooms are off to the right, Alina's are to the left, with a living room in the middle.

Eli keeps his arm around Liv but reaches out and extends a hand my way. "I'm Eli. The oldest Baker. Nice to meet you."

"You too, man." I plant my hand in his and give a firm shake. I'm not going to be scared by a big brother act. He may be the same height as me, and he appears in good physical shape, by the fact that he's broad shouldered and trim, but I have no issue with him if he has no issue with me.

The way Liv is holding on to him, she clearly has love for her brother. With a squeeze, she pushes off from him and curls into my side. I wrap my arm around her and kiss the top of her head, causing Eli and Alina to smile, and Mazie to scowl even deeper.

I gesture a hand in Mazie's direction. "You must be Mazie. Liv has told me a lot about you."

She examines my extremity like it's a foreign object before placing her hand in mine and shaking firmly. It's clear she's going to be the one I have to win over.

It makes sense for them to be so protective of not just Liv, but of each other. While I don't know the specifics of what they've been through, I can tell by Liv's behavior that it's catastrophic. Adding heartbreak only makes it worse. But I have zero intention of breaking Liv's heart.

There's a conversation to be had between us that we've certainly both been putting off. But she's worth finding a way to make things work for. What that would look like, I haven't the foggiest idea. But it's worth it.

"Dinner's almost ready. About another ten minutes. Liv, Jameson, can I get either of you a drink?"

"Anything, LeeLee. Anything." Liv presses herself closer into my side, though I didn't think it was possible.

I squeeze her even tighter. "I'm good with whatever you have, Alina. Thank you."

"Well, at least he has manners," Mazie grumbles.

"Mazie!" Liv whips her head around to look at her sister, but I just rub my hand up and down her side. I've faced worse. I've been called a dozen names in my field of work, mostly when I can't keep a business open.

"I brought some local beer if you'd like to give that a try. It's pretty good." Eli tries to throw me a bone, but as the big brother, I'm not sure what his game plan could be. Is he going to take me out back and have the "what are your intentions with my sister" talk? Or is that more likely to come from Mazie?

"Sure. That sounds great." I try to disengage myself from Liv, but she won't budge, holding impossibly tight around my waist.

I bend to her ear so only she can hear me. "Baby, if you want me to make a good impression, you need to let me go."

She turns her face so she can talk lowly back to me. "I'm trying to save you from the lions. I'm their tamer. Sort of."

A laugh erupts from my mouth, and I'm met with daggers. "It's going to be okay. I promise." Wrapping my hands around her biceps, I pull her from me and rest her hands at her sides. Her childishness is showing through, but it has to be hard in this family. She didn't necessarily get the chance to *be* a kid. At least that was the message I got from Seth the one day he let slip that something happened when they were young.

I follow Eli into the kitchen, where he opens the fridge and hands me a green can. "These are brewed about a half hour from here. They're pretty good."

"You live in Pineville City, right?"

"I do." He cracks open his can with a little more force than necessary.

"How'd you swing that? Seems like you guys all had to stay here."

"Liv say that?" He takes a sip as he eyes me over the can.

"Not in so many words. But I know she wants to get out of here and won't. I kind of assumed it was some unwritten rule." I take a swig of my beer. It's surprisingly good. An IPA and local. Hm. I wonder if Seth sells this at the store.

"Being the oldest has some perks. But mostly, it's close to my job. I work at the local college."

"Yeah, Liv mentioned that. Hell of an operation they have going on here with the café."

A smile spans his face. "Mazie will be pleased to hear that."

"I'll be pleased to hear what?"

"Jameson here thinks you guys have something great going with the café." He leans against the counter and crosses his feet at the ankle while Mazie comes and stands next to him. The resemblance is uncanny.

But where Eli is meeting me with a friendly look, Mazie's is anything but.

"Does he now? I guess based on his job, he does have some authority to know what he's talking about." There's utter disdain dripping off her words.

"I was just saying I think you'd done a good job getting it up and running and it seems to be doing well. Have you thought about having business-dependent merchandise? Like sellable mugs or t-shirts or the like with your brand and logo on them?"

Her brows tic up, and for the first time, she looks impressed instead of hateful. But it's short-lived.

"I haven't. That's not a bad idea, though." I'll take it as a compliment, since I'm sure it's the closest I'm going to get all night.

"Get out here! Now! All of you!" While I've never heard Liv use that tone before, I can tell she's *pissed*.

All three of us walk back into the living room, where she's standing with her arms across her chest and one foot tapping against the floor. I go right over to her and wrap my arm around her waist. "It's okay, baby."

"No interrogations tonight. Either one of you." She completely ignores me and waves a finger between Eli and Mazie, who both put on an innocent face.

"We're just getting to know each other, Bibly." Interesting nickname. They seem to have a lot that they switch to randomly. It'll be hard to keep up. Mazie acts like she hasn't been shooting daggers my way since I walked in the door.

"Not on my watch, Zee. Now, let's sit, since Alina said the food's almost done."

Though Liv is the baby of the family, she's fierce and mighty. And the other Baker siblings all know it. Crossing her doesn't seem like a good idea. I can easily see her throwing clothes out a third story window and not thinking twice about it.

She links her fingers through mine and pulls me to the table, sitting on the side with two chairs. Immediately, she scoots her chair closer and slinks under my arm so she can snuggle into my side. Though I can't see it, I have no doubt she's glaring at Mazie, who sits across from us.

And Mazie's stare seems glued on Liv. They're stuck in some sort of contest, and I look over at Eli, wondering what we should do. He lifts a hand and shakes his head, my indicator that we do nothing.

Alina breaks the tension by bringing in the most incredible smelling and looking lasagna I've ever seen, setting it down on a trivet in the middle of the table.

I stand to serve at the same time Eli does. With a wave of my hand, I sit back down, letting him take the lead. It's his family, after all.

He cuts everyone a slice and serves the side salad Alina brought out as well. Then Eli sits at one head of the table and Alina at the other. I have a feeling that Eli always sits at the head, and then whoever's house it is sits on the other side. That seems like a way this family would operate.

Though in my time with Liv I haven't taken her as religious, I do wait a beat before diving into my food to make sure they're not a family that says any sort of prayer before eating. When everybody else takes their first bite, I do too.

"Mmm" can be heard all around the table.

"This is delicious, Alina. Thank you for having me for dinner tonight." Manners will hopefully score me more points.

But Mazie's gaze is trained on me again, and it's angry.

"Here's the thing, Jameson. I don't trust you." Liv's fork clanks onto her plate at Mazie's sudden declaration.

"Okay. I can see why you might not. But I'll never hurt Liv."

"You're here temporarily, no?" Mazie has stopped eating and clasps her fingers in front of her.

"I am." Gently, I set my fork down, anticipating a longer conversation.

"So how do you expect her to not be hurt after you leave if you two continue down the path you're on?"

"That's a discussion we'll have to have." And not at this very moment.

"We won't let you take her away from us."

"Mazie," Liv angrily growls.

"I'd never dream of moving Liv from you all." Though why, I don't know. She's an adult, a big girl now. If she wants to move, she should be able to. Maybe it's backward. Maybe I should be arguing that I won't let them make her feel bad for wanting to move with me.

"I just don't see how that's going to work." She folds her arms against the table as she shrugs, flips her auburn hair over her shoulder, and rolls her sapphire eyes. Her whole attitude is that the conversation is over.

"With all due respect, isn't that up to me and Liv to decide?"

Mazie smiles what's surely a fake smile and looks down at the table for a moment before her eyes blaze on mine. "You've walked into a unique situation here, Jameson. But let's just say that it's up to me, and Eli, and Alina to protect Liv. To take care of her and make sure she's making the right decisions."

"I'm not a child anymore, Mazie. I can make my own life choices. Even if they may hurt in the end."

Mazie relaxes her glare on me and turns with a softer gaze to Liv. "I know you are, Bibly, but we're trying to look out for you. We're worried you're too blinded to see what's really going on here. What's really at stake."

"And you all feel this way?" There's a sadness in Liv's voice that makes me clench my jaw.

Mazie nods solemnly, while Eli and Alina have a look that tells me they don't necessarily agree but won't go against Mazie.

"Well, then. If that's the case, we'll get out of your hair. Come on, Jameson." Liv wipes her mouth and stands, extending a hand in my direction.

I do the same, standing and placing my napkin on the table. "Thank you, Alina. It was truly nice to meet you all."

Liv tugs my hand toward the front door, fire on her heels. She's done, and she's not going to wait for me.

I follow her right out the front door and to the car, where she stomps her foot and screams, looking up at the sky.

"What the fuck right do they think they have to say such things to you? To us. None. That's what right they have."

Cupping her cheeks, I press her against the car, taking her chin in my hand and turning her face to meet mine. "Hey. It's fine, Liv. Let them think what they want. We know what this is. Yes, there is a conversation we need to have, but we'll have it when *we* are ready. Not by their pushing."

I watch as the steam leaves her body and she goes lax, nodding at my suggestion.

"Now, let's get back to your place, and grab a pizza on the way, 'cause I'm starving."

Liv laughs as she climbs into the Corvette. I close the door behind her and take one last look back at the house filled with people I'm going to need to convince I'm good enough for their baby sister.

Chapter 17
Liv

The shrill ring of the phone causes my eyes to pop open. Trying to get up, I have the heavy weight of Jameson's arm across my middle. He groans as I move it off me.

"Who's calling this late at night? Ignore it." His voice is leaden with sleep.

But I can't ignore it, because only one person calls this late. Before the ringing even stops, I'm already out of bed and pulling on pants. Putting on my bra, I frantically glance around, looping my hair behind my ears as I look for a shirt.

"Liv, what are you doing? Come back to bed. It's three in the morning." With his eyes still closed, he reaches across the bed in my general direction.

"Um, I can't. I have to go. Shirt. I need a shirt." Frantically, I look around the room for any article of clothing that may be a top.

"Go? Where are you going?" That gets him to open his eyes and lean up on his elbows.

Tugging on whatever cotton material I find on the floor, I move over to the bed and give Jameson a quick peck.

"I have to go. I'll explain later."

Before he can even respond, I'm dashing out the door, grabbing my keys on the way out, and slamming the door shut behind me.

Jameson's been staying with me for three weeks, and in that time, we've been lucky to avoid a night like tonight.

Letting myself into the house, I'm met with darkness and silence. Before I even have my shoes off, the scream echoes down the hall and I take off running.

Getting to her room, I climb on the bed and wrap my arms tightly around her. "Shh, LeeLee, it's me, it's Liv. Shh, you're okay."

Holding my sister in my arms, I rock her gently from side to side while I run my hand over her chocolate tresses. This happens once in a while. She wakes enough to call me, and then falls asleep again while she waits.

We keep swaying and shushing, and at a certain point, I start humming. Eventually, the sobs turn to hitches and the shaking stops.

"You need to get help, Leen. This can't keep happening. I can't keep doing this." The only indication I have that she's awake enough to hear me is the fact that her fingers are fiddling with a rip in my pants.

"You smell different."

Looking down at myself, I see that the shirt I grabbed is Jameson's. Pulling back, Alina looks me over. And then her face drops and her bottom lip starts to tremble. "You were with Jameson. I pulled you away from him. I'm sorry, Liv, I'm so sorry."

"Alina, you need *help*. I love you, you know I am always here for you, but we can't keep doing this. I can't keep being the one who rescues you in the middle of the night." I'm pleading with her in the same way I have a million times. And I know it's going to fall on deaf ears like it always does.

"You know that Mazie will try to convince me to move in with her. And I can't ask Eli to drive that far." Eli's the only one of us who doesn't live within the confines of Juniper Grove. It's not that he's terribly far, it's just more than the ten minutes it takes me or would take Mazie to get here.

Our town is small, but it can still take a half hour to get from end to end if you hit the lights wrong or if there's traffic. You're less likely to encounter that in the middle of the night, but still. Alina lives mostly in the central part of town, while I'm on the eastern side and Mazie's on the west. Eli lives in Pineville City.

"That's not what I mean, Alina. You need to be able to save *yourself*. You need help." She needs a therapist. It's likely we all do, but she's the only one who has these sorts of episodes. At least that I know of.

Pushing away from me, I know I said the one thing she doesn't want to hear. "I'm fine."

"You're *not*. Alina, please. I love you. I can't keep seeing you like this." I take her hand in both of mine and try to get her to make eye contact with me.

Smoothing her hair back, she refuses to even look at me, her eyes trained on the corner of her room.

"It's been years, LeeLee. Years. This isn't sustainable."

"It hasn't been that long." She picks at her sleeve, the cuff of which she's pulled into her fist.

This is the point we reach when I know there's no talking to her; there's no convincing her that she needs more than what I can do for her.

Sliding off the bed, I stand and run my hand down the front of my pants, eyes trained on my feet. "Okay, well, you seem to be better now. I'm going to go home and try to get a few more hours of sleep. I'll see you at the café later."

"Sure."

I hate when we leave things like this. Neither one of us ever knows how the other feels. I'm worried about her to the point that I'll go home and *not* sleep another wink, going through all the possibilities and all the things we should be doing for her. Eli and Mazie have no idea the extent of it. She doesn't want them to, and I haven't wanted to rat her out.

Maybe it's time that ship sails.

Dragging myself back to my place, I find Jameson sitting up in bed, awake, and scrolling through his phone, which he quickly shuts off and tosses to the side when I enter.

He throws his arms around his drawn-up knees and heaves a sigh as he gives me a quick once over.

Climbing up on the bed, I scuttle close to him, leaning my head against his shoulder. It's been such a short period of time, but he's become a comfort to me.

As he wraps his arm around me, he tugs me into his side and lies back on the bed, bringing me down with him.

"Talk." With a single word, he starts twirling my curls through his fingers. It's calming in the truest sense of the word. Just *being* with Jameson is calming in a way nothing else ever has been. But when he takes my hair in his hand, all the tension oozes from my body.

"It was Alina." Swallowing around the lump in my throat, I know the conversation I've been avoiding has finally arrived. "She was having a nightmare. When we lived together, it was easy because she was just down the hall. But now, when she's awake enough, she calls me instead."

"How long has she been having them?"

"Years. And she refuses to get help. They were better for a while she was with—"

There's an inability to finish that sentence, to even utter the name. Shaking my head, I continue without it. "There was a period of time when she wasn't having them. But when that ended, they came back even worse than before."

While I don't want to leave the warm and comforting cocoon of Jameson's arms, I need to be able to look at him while I have this conversation. Pushing up to sitting, I cross my legs, knotting my fingers in my lap and locking my eyes on them.

Jameson's large, warm hands envelop my own and bring my knuckles to his lips. A tear patters against my jeans.

"Whatever you have to say, Liv, I'm here for you."

"I know, which is why I'm going to tell you. I need you to know, first, that I've never told anybody else this story before. We haven't talked about our feelings, or what we're doing here besides, I don't know, playing house. But you need to know that you're the only person I've ever felt comfortable having this conversation with." I still can't look at him, but I know he knows me well enough by now to believe that I mean it. Or at the very least, he hears the seriousness in my voice.

Taking one hand from the pile, he tips my chin up. Looking up at him through my damp eyelashes, I find sincerity sweeping through his dazzling silvers.

"You're right. We haven't talked about our feelings. So hear me, right now. I'm falling in love with you, Liv. I look forward to leaving work and coming home to you. That's never happened to me before. Nobody has ever taken priority above my job before. Only you."

Warmth starts in my heart and spreads throughout my entire body as my shoulders sag from relief. "I'm falling in love with you too." The words come out on a whispered breath.

Cupping the back of my neck, he pulls my head to his and rests our foreheads together for a moment before leaning in and brushing his lips against mine. When he sits back, I immediately want him to return.

"Please talk to me. Let me know what happened, what's going on, how I can help."

"First of all, it's sweet that you want to help, but you can't. Nobody can." Taking a deep breath, I do my best to steel myself for what lies ahead.

"You've heard that there's something surrounding me and my siblings. But you don't know what. We were all really close growing up, with my parents too. We were a happy group. We enjoyed spending time together, even with my parents, despite being teenagers." A chill runs through my body. I don't think I've said the word "parents" at all in the past few years and I just said it twice in a thirty-second span.

"Alina's been my best friend my whole life. And not just because we're sisters. I'd choose her even if we weren't related. Eli has this ability to be there for all of us when we need him, always has. It's like he's a chameleon and can change himself to be who we need at the time." I leave Mazie out, partially on purpose, partially because our relationship has always been the rockiest.

Closing my eyes, I tilt my head toward the ceiling. "When I was thirteen, my parents were murdered, right here in town."

I hear Jameson's sharp inhalation of breath and practically feel his heart skip. It does right along with my own.

"It was a stranger, somebody passing through town, who according to police was high out of his mind and tried carjacking them, but it went wrong, or at least that's what we were told. How they know, I haven't a clue. They were out on a date one minute, then bleeding out in the street the next."

He wipes a stray tear from my cheek. After all these years, I've tried to lock away the emotions that come with even thinking about this story. But I knew I was going to have to tell him at some point and I tried to steal myself for this conversation.

"We've always stayed together because of that. I'm the youngest of four, Alina was fifteen, almost sixteen. They all had to take care of me...we had to take care of each other. It strengthened our already strong connection. Sure, there were bad times, hard times. Mazie fell into the role of Mom very seamlessly, but was still a teenager herself, on track for college. Mostly only because she didn't have a choice. We have no other family, since my parents were both only children, whose parents had passed on years before they did. They had no backup plan for us, because they didn't know who they could trust us with."

Jameson squeezes my hands, but I can barely feel it. All I can feel is the ache settled in my chest and the sting behind my eyes.

"If it wasn't for Mazie and Eli, Alina and I would have ended up in foster care. Or at the very least, I would have. Instead, we both finished high school. We stayed in the house until I graduated, then quickly sold it. We had inherited all their money, then whatever we got from the sale of the house. Splitting it four ways still left us each with a substantial amount. Enough to later buy our business.

"While I finished school here, Mazie attended the local college to get her MBA so she could open her own business one day. Alina was always cooking, even before our parents. She went to college and studied culinary arts. While there, she fell in love with baking, of all things." It's a good thing because it's lead us to what we have, where we are and how we survive.

"We all started to drink a lot of coffee after, especially me. I was trying to keep up with my siblings, who always thought I was young and naive and didn't pay attention. But I did. I saw their struggles. Money wasn't really a problem, but I still tried to help where I could."

The sting behind my eyes becomes too much and they overflow, our hands being splattered with salty water. Jameson cups my cheek, swiping his thumb under my eye. He's been silent this whole time, absorbing every word and letting me voice my innermost feelings, and now, demons.

"I got a little wild as I got older. The rebellious stage...let's just say, I hit it *hard*. Eli had to come get me from many parties because I was drunk. The first one was when I was fifteen. Throughout the years, I may have started a fight or two, got caught having sex in a bedroom at a party." Glancing at him, his eyebrows are almost at his hairline.

"Yeah, I'm not proud of it. But I was going through a rough time, and I didn't have my parents to talk to. There were some days I wanted nothing more than to just curl up in my mom's lap and talk to her about my day, the boy I liked, anything. Mazie, as protective as she was, wasn't that type of support. Alina, while older, doesn't have the sage advice of a mom. I was lost. So, I acted out." My shoulders sag with the weight of what I was like as a teenager.

"That makes sense, Liv. You had a horrible thing happen to you, all of you. It's understandable to react the way you did. You were a kid."

"You think I'm still a kid." I lift my eyes to his with a half smile on my face, even though it practically pains me to have it there.

"You know what I mean."

"Regardless, when I turned eighteen, I moved out. I found an apartment and Alina moved in with me when she came home from college. That's when I first learned about her nightmares. The three of us put our money in to buy the shop and open the café, with Mazie running the back end, and Alina doing the baking, I was nominated to run the front and handle a lot of the coffee duties."

Sliding his hands to my hips, Jameson grips tightly and pulls me into his lap so I'm straddling him. Brushing the hair from my face and cupping my ears, he looks me over, searching my face for an answer to an unasked question.

"I lied to you before, Liv. I'm not falling in love with you. I already have. I love you. This story, everything you've told me tonight, it just makes me realize just how strong you are. You're wonderful and amazing, and I knew it since day one, but this just solidifies it and shows me why."

Everything in my body stills. The shadow of numbness that shrouds me when I think about my parents, or the very little bit I talk about them, ebbs away and allows the light of Jameson's words to sneak in and cover me in a warm, safe blanket. My blood flows with newfound vigor, my heartbeats and breaths have purpose.

"I love you too."

Moving a hand to the back of my head, Jameson pulls my mouth to his briefly.

"We opened the café because it was my parents' dream to own a shop of some sort. It changed all the time. Sometimes it was a bookstore, sometimes it was a home goods store, sometimes it was a pet shop, even though we never had a pet growing up. But with Alina's affinity for baking and mine for coffee, we decided a café was the best thing. Not to mention, our town was in desperate need of one. We never expected it to become such an establishment, but it has." We figured we'd go bankrupt within the first six months. But our town showed up for us. It helps that we have good products too.

"What you three have done is incredible."

"This town is really to thank. They did what they could when everything happened, but it wasn't much. They've always supported us, though, come in regularly and always tell the tourists that we're the best cup of coffee for miles."

"No, Sweetheart. You Bakers did that all on your own."

I lean into Jameson's chest, and he wraps his arms around me and kisses my forehead. Exhaustion weighs down my eyelids and body. It's more mental and emotional than physical.

Keeping me against him, he leans back to the bed. Laying on top of him, hearing his heart beating under my ear and his arms tight around me, is the safest I've felt in a long time, possibly ever.

"Sleep, baby, I'm here with you."

It's the last thing I hear before sleep overtakes me.

Chapter 18

Jameson

Liv zonked out on me at least ten minutes ago, but I can't possibly move from underneath her. It's kind of nice, having her this close. Usually, we just lie next to each other and drift apart before one of us seeks the other out. But feeling her weight adds a new level of intensity.

I knew it was something terrible she wouldn't talk about, *couldn't* talk about. But I never could have imagined it was anything on this level.

My poor girl, she's been through so much. The whole family has. That's another thing, she never said the word "family" or any variation of "die". You can tell it's still too hard for her.

Squeezing her a little tighter, I kiss the top of her head. It wasn't my intention to tell her I love her tonight. I wasn't even sure I was going to tell her. The falling part, yeah, that I figured would come out. But I planned to keep the fact that I already fell to myself. It will be muddier now. I'm still only here temporarily.

I can't change it, though, and I don't want to. Because despite the fact that my time here is limited, I don't want my time with Liv to be. I've already dragged out a lot of what I have to do with Seth, extending how long it takes to do things. Instead of staying until all hours of the night, or working through it, I'm leaving no later than six and coming home to her. Because her home feels like my own.

She's welcomed me in, given me a key, had me check out of the motel. This life, the relationship and sharing my space with somebody, was not something I wanted, or thought I'd have. I've been single for years and embraced my life alone. But with Liv? It seems impossible to think of ever being in solitude again.

When Liv starts to stir, I loosen my arms and look down. But she's not waking up, just snuggling in closer.

I want this every day, every night.

Never once have I had a thought like that. In just a few weeks, Liv has become the most important part of my life. I'll have to figure out how to make this work with my career.

Maybe I *can* get her to move with me. Liv's talked about loving the city, wanting to live there someday. I know she doesn't want to leave her siblings, but it doesn't mean she can't, right?

Before I have a chance to think too much about it, she jumps up, straddling me and blinking quickly. I slide my hands down her back to rest on her upper thighs.

"Good morning, beautiful."

"I fell asleep." Her violet eyes are wide with the realization, and she continues to give big, sleepy blinks.

"Yeah, you did." I run my hands up and down her thighs as I take in all her beauty.

"I don't usually fall asleep when I come back from Alina's."

"You shared a lot."

"Yeah," she sighs. "I think I was just really comfortable."

"Good. I'm glad."

"Did you mean it?" Despite the fact that it's only been a few weeks, I know Liv well enough to know what this *it* is.

Tucking some hair behind her ear, I run my fingers down her jaw to hold her chin. "Every word."

Her head dips down and her hair brushes my chest. Reaching behind me, I adjust the pillow to be against the headboard. Wrapping my arm around Liv's waist, I push myself back so I can sit up and pull her into my chest. She folds instantly, curling her arms in between us.

When her breaths even out, I wonder if she fell asleep again, but then her voice floats up, quiet and nervous. "Say it again."

With a smile pulling the corners of my lips up high, I repeat the words I know she wants to hear. "I love you."

A hum vibrates from her body into mine. "I love you too."

My heart skips a beat, and when Liv giggles, I'm sure it's because she heard it.

"I have to go to work." Ending on a whine, she buries her face in my chest, and I can't help but laugh. The behavior seems childlike in a way, but it's endearing all the same.

"Because you don't want to leave me, or because you don't want to see your sister?"

Leaning up, she meets my gaze with a sheepish look on her face. "Both?"

"Well, if it makes you feel better, I have to go to work too, and don't feel like leaving this nice, warm nest we have either."

"You'll be home for dinner?"

"Yeah, I'll be home for dinner." I hook some hair behind her ear, and she leans into my touch, kissing my palm.

The thought of being home for dinner is a strange one. It's something you'd say to a life partner. And that's something I never really expected to have. Sure, I've always figured at some point I'll be lonely and settle down with somebody who is good enough. But I never expected somebody to take my breath away like Liv has.

And the whole world can tell.

When I get to the store, Seth takes one look at me, and a smile spans his face. "You look...happy. For the first time since I've met you. Liv Baker has done you in, hasn't she?"

My brow furrows together. "How'd you know?"

"Seen you at the café with her once or twice. But you, my friend, are a man in love and I can tell. I've been with my wife for over thirty years."

I flop into the chair and put my hand to my lip. "I don't know what I'm doing, Seth. I leave in a few short weeks. Really, I could leave at almost any time because we're doing good work here, and you're on the track to profit now. How can I be so foolish as to fall in love with somebody here?"

"Matters of the heart don't always make sense."

"Yeah, but I'm pulling her along with me. That's not fair to her."

"Well, if our time here really is coming to a close, I'd consider how you want to broach that with her. That one, she's a firecracker. I know I've said that before, but I'm not sure you've fully seen it in her yet." While her personality certainly fits, and she's got the spunk, the way he says it makes me a little nervous.

There are certainly things about the other we haven't seen yet, haven't experienced. But the way he's talking, I'm not sure I *want* to see that side of Liv.

"Is it messy?"

"There was one time, when she was living in the apartments, she caught a boyfriend cheating on her and threw all his belongings out of her third-floor window. Didn't even really yell a ton, just threw his things and him out and that was it."

Even having thought it at some point, my eyes widen in surprise. Liv had mentioned the cheating boyfriend, somebody who she thankfully said left town because I'd ring his damn neck. But she failed to mention her retaliation.

I'd never betray Liv. But would she look at me leaving as just that, though? Would she take it out on me in the same way?

The conversation we've been avoiding seems to be looming nearer and nearer.

Chapter 19
Liv

Getting to the café today, I'm not sure what to expect. Alina and I rarely leave things like we did last night.

The thunk of the lock rolling into the open position makes me flinch and my eyes flutter closed. I have no reason to be jumpy, because I'm not wrong.

Tossing my bag under the counter, I perk my ears up for the familiar sounds of the mixer, pans scraping the oven racks. But I don't find any. Did Alina not show up for work today?

Rushing through the door, I find her huddled over the counter. A mixture of scents waft in my direction. She got a head start, which means she was here early. Which, in turn, means she didn't go back to sleep after I left.

"Oh, LeeLee."

She lifts her face and I see the dark circles, the deep creases, and even the stained lines from her tears. My heart drops to my feet and with it, all the blood follows.

"I'm okay." The words are entirely unconvincing and I'm wondering if she's starting to not believe herself.

"You're *not*. You can't keep going like this." I'm surprised exhaustion hasn't landed her in the hospital, and I'm convinced if she keeps going this way it will.

"I have four dozen muffins in the oven; blueberry, cinnamon crunch, coffee cake, and Dutch chocolate. Scones will be going in shortly. There's still carrot cake, brownies, and fudge from yesterday." Avoidance. Her favorite tactic.

"How long have you been here?"

"A few hours."

Neither of us knows what to say and we look awkwardly around the room.

"Sorry for pulling you away from Jameson last night. I hope he wasn't too mad when you got back."

"You guys don't seem to care to understand him at all. He's not like that. He was worried, not angry." The frustration in my voice isn't the most appropriate knowing her state of mind at the moment, but I'm tired of nobody giving him the benefit of the doubt.

Alina picks up on this and holds her hands up in peace. "Whoa, I'm not against him, Liv. I think it would make sense for him to be mad that you're leaving in the middle of the night."

"Maybe you could try to get to know him a little, instead of judging."

"Liv, really, I'm not judging. And I think that's a good idea. Actually, wait, why didn't he come in with you?" The past two weeks he's been coming with me in the morning, adding a second dose of coffee to his daily routine.

"I thought it'd be better if I came alone first. I wasn't quite sure where we stood."

Closing the gap in a few steps, Alina wraps her arms around me and squeezes tight. It takes me a second to return the gesture. "You're my sister, Liv, and I love you. It doesn't matter what we say or what happens, we are always good. Okay?"

Nodding against her, I swallow back the lump and burning behind my eyes. "I'm just worried about you."

"I know. I'm sorry."

"I can't be the one who keeps helping you, Lee." She lets go of me and wipes her hands on her apron.

"I'm just going to focus on these."

With a growl, I turn around and head back to the café. I can bring it up a million times and she's never going to respond to me the way I need her to. Sometimes I'm convinced the only person who can make the nightmares better is the one who did the first time. But that was a long time ago, and he's long gone.

I'm not out front for more than five minutes before the bell rings and Jameson strolls through the door. A smile pulls up the corners of my lips and he makes a beeline for me, wrapping me in his arms and kissing the top of my head.

From the embrace, you'd think we haven't seen each other in hours instead of a mere forty-five minutes.

"Hey, baby. How'd things go?" His deep voice rumbles through my ear and straight to my heart.

"Not great. She just refuses to see that she needs more help than I can give her. I don't know what to do at this point."

His hand runs down my hair and back on repeat as we sway slightly. "Mind if I talk to her?"

I lean back, keeping my arms wrapped around his waist. "You?"

"Yes, me."

"Why?" My eyes widen, and I rest my hands on his chest. "Sorry, that was rude. I'm just surprised."

"There was a time I had some trouble sleeping. It wasn't quite insomnia, and I needed to seek professional help. It can be tough. I'd like to see if I can help. I love you, Sweetheart. And you're worried about your sister. Which means *I'm* worried about your sister."

I'm not really sure what to think of this suggestion. While I appreciate that he's concerned about her too, I don't know that he needs to be. Is that what being in love means?

"What's the worst that could happen?" He has a point.

"I mean, I guess. If she's willing to talk to you, that is. I'm not going to force it." Maybe talking to him will be what she needs to seek help. To find a way to help herself.

"Neither would I."

"I'll go tell her." I slip from his hold and disappear into the kitchen, but she's nowhere to be found. "LeeLee?"

I nearly jump out of my skin as she pokes up from behind the counter. "Sorry. Cleaning up a mess."

From the looks of it, she spilled flour. Again. It's all in her hair and smudged on her face. I wish this wasn't such a frequent occurrence. So does Mazie.

"What's up?" She bends to continue cleaning up the mess she made.

"Jameson wants to talk to you."

The way she straightens with her eyebrows high on her head, you'd think I said he wanted to marry her instead of just have a conversation. "Me?"

With my mouth pressed into a line, I nod.

"Um. Okay."

Though I'm not giving her the full picture, I think it might be best to avoid telling her what about.

The second we leave the kitchen, Jameson smiles, gives me a quick kiss on the forehead, and leads Alina over to a table, far enough away from me that I can't hear their hushed voices.

They lean in toward each other and talk back and forth. I'm not a good enough lip reader to know what's being said and won't eavesdrop. Jameson surely picked that table on purpose.

It's strange to watch them together. They seem to get along well enough. Alina's the only one who hasn't expressed any concerns about him, but that doesn't mean they'd get along.

None of it matters to me. Just my relationship with Jameson.

I can barely take my eyes off them as they continue to have their secret conversation. But when Alina flops back in her chair and crosses her arms with a huff, I straighten, ready to go on the defensive. I love Jameson, but that's my sister.

It doesn't seem necessary though, as Jameson says something and Alina nods before they both stand and come back over, Alina heading straight into the kitchen.

"She's going to be okay, Liv. It may take time. She knows what she needs to do; she's just scared. But she knows you're here."

"That's all I get?"

"'Fraid so." Leaning down, he brushes his lips against mine. "I have to get to work. But I'll come by at my normal time. I love you."

"I love you too." With one more quick kiss, he's off. And I'm left to wonder what the hell that conversation was all about.

Chapter 20
Jameson

The conversation I had with Alina this morning keeps replaying in my mind. She knows she needs help, and she knows she can't keep calling Liv, but she's scared and is used to having a crutch.

She said something about how they tend to come in spurts, clusters. I wonder what she'd do if Liv wasn't around?

Maybe I should make that happen? We could go away for the weekend. I know she's dying to see the city. I could take her away for a few days, and we could stay in my apartment. Give her a taste of what her life could be like if she moved with me, which is something I'm absolutely prepared to ask her to do. The whole concept is foreign and seems out of left field, but it's impossible not to feel that way about Liv.

While I'm fairly certain the answer will be no, because of needing to be close to her siblings, I have to take the shot.

"You're distracted today." Seth's become far more observant of me and my behavior since I started dating Liv. I think this whole town watches out for that family.

"Yeah, I had an interesting conversation this morning."

"I keep telling you, Liv's a firecracker."

"Actually, it was with Alina."

His eyebrows go skyward. "Oh. I mean, she's had a rough go as well, outside their family. I take it you know about their parents by now?"

"Yeah, Liv just told me last night."

"After all the time you two have been together and she just told you? I didn't realize it was still so hard for them to talk about." He says the last part almost to himself as he looks away.

"They all still seem very much affected by it. Which is quite understandable."

Seth nods in agreement but seems lost in his own head. I wonder if he knew Liv's parents, their family, before it fell apart. In such a small town, I imagine everybody did on some level.

"We're going to take this weekend off. I want to give Liv some time away. So, no business this weekend." I already talked to Alina about taking Liv down to the city at some point; I just didn't expect it to be so soon. But after our conversation, it needs to happen now.

"Alright. That sounds fine. Can we afford to do that?"

"Things are moving in the right direction. And if I'm being completely honest with you, I'm stalling for more time with Liv. I could have left a week or two ago, and things would continue on their track. But I want to see it through and be with Liv as long as possible." Longer than possible, really. There are things I need to attend to at home.

Yet lately, the thought of home feels so foreign and lonely. Liv's house is more like home to me these days.

"Okay. Sounds like a weekend off to me. The missus will be pleased to hear it."

A smile spans my face. His wife is a good woman who supports and adores her husband. Something I find myself wanting more and more. And not with just anybody, but with Liv and Liv alone.

One way to possibly make that work is to have her move with me. I have to show her the city, show her what she's missing by refusing to leave Juniper Grove.

The only step now is convincing her to take the weekend away with me.

Chapter 21
Liv

Jameson's Battery Park City apartment is nothing short of jaw dropping. Floor-to-ceiling windows line the living room, giving a breathtaking view of the Hudson River and parts of New Jersey. It's like my body can't control the momentum and I'm drawn right to it.

"Wow." The word is barely a wisp of air as my fingertips graze the glass, lightly, as though it may shatter in front of me.

"Beautiful, isn't it?" His arm wraps around my waist, fingers dipping into the front of my jeans, while his lips graze my neck.

"Extremely."

His other hand glides up my body, wrapping around my throat and tipping my head back against his shoulder.

"Jameson," I whisper.

His responding growl against my neck has me squeezing my thighs together.

When he sprung it on me earlier in the week that he wanted to take me to see his stomping ground, I was a little shocked, to say the least.

My initial protests of not being able to leave work were quickly shot down by Alina, who not only said she called in reinforcements, but swore they'd be fine. We technically do have a staff, albeit a small one, who are great at their job. It's just that we all typically prefer to be as hands on as possible.

Jameson was quick to step in and insist that we could come back if there was any sign of trouble, or if I was needed, but he had to head back to handle a few things and really wanted me to join him. And I've always wanted to go to New York City. Saying no wasn't even an option.

Right now, as his lips caress from my ear to my shoulder, and one hand slides into my pants while the city bustles below us, I'm eternally happy I said yes.

"None of those people down there know that I'm about to fuck you in this apartment. It's a crazy notion, isn't it?"

Just looking down at the block below us, it's busier than all of Juniper Grove.

So far, I love everything about the city, and we've barely been here an hour. We drove down in the Corvette and came straight to Jameson's apartment.

While this is far from the city experience I'd have on my own, I can already tell it's going to be an amazing visit.

"I need you to come back to me, Liv."

With a quick shake of my head, I turn in Jameson's grasp, pushing up on my toes to connect our mouths. "Sorry. If you didn't want me to be distracted, you shouldn't have shown me the view."

"You're the best view around. I forget sometimes that the city is impressive. Especially to somebody new. I promise to show you all the sights, but not before I get a chance to fuck you in my bed."

Not another word is spoken as he hoists me over his shoulder, smacking my ass and striding down the hall. My last view is the bobbing cityscape behind us.

Jameson climbs on the bed before flipping me and dropping me beneath him. His fingers start loosening his tie immediately, and I lie here, taking in the delicious view of my man undressing, with eyes that are full of lust and need. I can barely sit still.

His tie is pulled from his neck, and before I can realize what he's doing, a one-sided grin takes over his face, and he's pulling my hands above my head. He loops the silken garment around the bed post before tying it around my wrists, which are already bound tightly together.

He trails his fingers down my arm as he bends and kisses along my collarbone and across my chest, straight to the exposed skin between my jeans and the hem of my shirt.

"Your youth shines through when you wear clothes that expose your midriff, Liv. But fuck if it doesn't drive me *wild*." Which is the exact reason I do it. Sure, I've been known to wear shirts that show off some skin, but with Jameson around, it's become a routine wardrobe choice.

His deepened tone skims my nerve endings, as his hands slip up the inside of my shirt. Both hands cup my breasts as his teeth pull at the fabric of my jeans, and he looks up at me from his spot practically between my thighs.

I wrap my legs around his waist, hooking them at the ankles. "Please, Jameson."

A gentle 'hmm' flutters across my skin and he pushes my shirt up to my chin, pulling down the cup of my bra and blowing on my left nipple. My back arches and my thighs clench as the skin pebbles from his gentle breath. The tip of his tongue gives one tiny flick at the flesh before pulling it into his mouth.

At the same time, he's lavishing my nipple, he unbuttons my jeans and slides his hand into my pants, his fingers slipping along my soaking pussy.

"Mmm, dear God, Liv. You're always so ready for me."

"For you? Of course I am." How could I not be? He knows exactly what to do to make my body sing. And it does time and time again, only for him.

With a quick bite at my nipple, I release a shriek that ends on a moan as he eases two fingers inside me. My head tips back, and my hands try to wrap around the silken tie keeping them above my head.

Despite being stuck, I writhe and wiggle beneath him as he uses his fingers expertly and presses tender kisses along my abdomen.

It's not until his mouth moves back to my breast and he swirls his tongue around my nipple that my hips lift off the mattress, chasing his hand, needing more and more until a whine tears from my lips.

"That's my girl." Moving away from me, he pulls my jeans and panties off, dropping them to the floor before quickly undressing himself. There's no tease of slowly unbuttoning his shirt, no ceremony to stand on.

I take an extra minute to drink him in while he stands in just his black boxer briefs, before they too are unceremoniously removed and tossed on the pile. Then desire courses through me at an increased rate, my lip planted firmly between my teeth.

He moves back over me slowly, like he's a tiger on the prowl, stalking his prey, though I'm stuck in place, so not much stalking is necessary.

"You're a vision, Liv. Especially underneath me."

"Not so bad yourself, Jameson." It's not just how he looks or how he hovers over me, but he cages me in completely. It's like there's no safer place than under him.

Without another word, he eases his length into me and my breath catches. What I wouldn't give for the use of my hands right now, but this is new and different and if he wants it, I'll do it.

He moves his hips slowly, and I already need more. More force, more speed...just more. I wriggle and try to get the message across, but I can tell by the half smirk on his face he knows exactly what he's by doing going slowly.

Letting anticipation build, taking his dear sweet time to torture me.

Which is why when he's all the way inside me, I wrap my legs tightly around his waist, holding him in place and grinding myself against him, my clit rubbing along his lower abs.

"Mmm, fuck, Jay. I need more."

He takes both of my legs, hooking my knees at his elbows so I'm wide open, and drives me into me hard and fast.

"Fuck, baby, you feel so damn good."

"So do you. Fuck. So good." And it's the damnedest truth. Nobody has ever felt as amazing as Jameson does and I know I'm ruined going forward, because nobody can ever compare.

My head tips to the side, giving him exposure to kiss up my neck, and I take in the skyline.

Part of me is sure he brought me here to possibly convince me to move with him. But he's going to learn why I can't do that. Why that's never going to be an option for me.

It's the dream I've always had, living here, finding somebody to spend that time with. I may have done it a bit backward, but the dream was never meant to be a reality.

The thing that's thrown a wrench in it all is the man currently fucking me to within an ounce of consciousness. I had resigned to a life in Juniper Grove, had come to terms with my reality and my future. But Jameson barreled into my life and started making me question things. Things that can't be changed.

"Where's your head at, Liv?"

"Everywhere." He's one person I've never lied to.

Lowering my legs, he leans down on his forearms and brushes some hair from my face while staying inside me. "Come back to me. Be in this moment with me."

I give my head a quick shake and try to come back, but there's just so much racing through my mind it's hard. "I'm trying. This is a lot."

"Do you want to stop?"

I move to wrap my arms around his shoulders before the tension reminds me that I'm tied up. "No. I don't know. I never not want to be having sex with you...it's just, there's a lot going through my head right now."

He kisses up along my neck as he pulls out and rolls to his side, untying my hands and turning me to face him.

"Talk to me, baby."

"Just, being here, in the city, all that comes through my mind when I think of it. What I've given up." A future that's what I wanted and have envisioned versus what I think it needs to be.

Quickly, I stand to get dressed. The conversation I was expecting to happen seems to be now. Jameson follows suit, pulling on his boxers and shirt, but leaving it unbuttoned.

"All of this can be yours, Liv. You can have this life. We can have it together. Move here...with me."

"I can't do that."

"Why not, Liv? You need to learn to live for yourself a little."

I push back from him, the anxiety and tears bubbling beneath the surface, and I rake my fingers through my curls. "I can't. I won't leave my siblings."

"Why? Eli did. No, he's not far, but he's not in that Godforsaken town either." His hand lands on my hip in a territorial way that I've come to love.

"You don't get it, Jameson. You couldn't possibly. Eli's different. He sacrificed *everything* for us. When my parents—when it happened, Eli was at MIT." His eyes widen. All I can do is nod and pull my lip between my teeth while looking at the ground. "It was his dream. Ever since he was old enough to know about college and what it means, he wanted to go to MIT. He had the brains to do it.

"The accident happened during Eli's freshman year. He came home and never went back. He didn't even go to pack up his belongings. He had his roommate do it and ship everything to us or toss it. He has a great job as a professor now, but he could be *so much more*." A sob breaks from my chest and my hand flies to my mouth as I fall to my knees.

My brother is an amazing human, and I could never in my life begin to repay him for the sacrifices he's made. Being the youngest, I know that many of those sacrifices were for my sole benefit. Mazie and Alina would have been fine, but I was barely a teenager, closer to a preteen, really, and he stopped his whole life to take care of me. The ache in my chest is so intense, I double over.

Jameson's arms wrap tightly around me, pulling me against him. Turning me into his chest, his lips graze the top of my head.

"It's okay, Liv, I've got you."

He holds me while I bawl against him, on the floor, in the middle of his bedroom. I'm sure this isn't what he had in mind for this weekend.

"I'm sorry. It's just…I can't leave them, Jameson. I need to be with my sisters, with my siblings. We're a unit. You get one, you get all of us. Even Eli, because he would drop everything if we needed him to. Not to mention, we do Sunday dinner."

It's something I've put on hold since Jameson came into my life, since he didn't get the warm welcome I was hoping. But every Sunday, we'd all get together for dinner, alternating whose house we were at. Alina doesn't always cook, but she does often end up bringing the main meal.

"I know, baby, it was just a thought. I want you to have everything you want in life. That city life? I can give it to you. I *want* to give it to you." And I know he does, beyond anything else. Especially because then we can continue to be together.

"Did I ever tell you how we opened the café?"

"No." His fingers glide lazily up and down my spine.

"It had been a dream of my parents. You'd asked me if we opened a café because of the last name Baker. Well, that may have been *their* intention, but it wasn't ours. We just wanted to honor their memory. There was a part of the business for us three sisters. And while we were willing to go into it just us three, Eli gave us most of his inheritance to help get the shop up and running."

This is the first time I've shared this story with another soul. Kylee lived it with me, but I've never actually told anybody. It feels like an impossibly heavy weight is finally lifting free from my chest.

"He sounds like a saint."

"I'm not entirely convinced he isn't. Jameson, I love my brother and sisters, more than you could possibly imagine and more than most siblings probably love one another. We have an untouchable, undeniable, and unbreakable bond. We went through something traumatic together.

That can do two things. It can tear people apart or bring them together. We were *sewn* together."

Leaning back, I put my hands against his chest and meet his eyes. "I love you, so much. As far as I'm concerned, you're my future. But I don't have a future with anybody who doesn't include my siblings in that, who doesn't understand our connection."

Running his hand down my hair, he nods slowly. "I do, of course, I do. It was stupid of me to even mention it. Like I said, Liv, I just want to be able to give you everything you've ever wanted. This? This is something I can give you."

Looking around the apartment, my heart stutters and my teeth clamp together. While this is everything I've wanted for most of my life, everything changed that one March night. Even if I still would love every aspect of this, I can't have it.

"I know. I do. I just, I can't."

Nodding and dropping his head, he cups the back of my neck, pulling my forehead to rest against his. "I love you."

"And I love you."

"Why don't we get ready and go have some dinner? Walk around a little bit and show you some of the city at night?"

"That sounds amazing."

The conversation I'd been somewhat dreading didn't turn out to be as terrible as I'd feared it would be. And I'm not sure why I was so nervous. Jameson is amazing and understanding and gets me in a way nobody else has. He never once blinked about the relationship, the connection I have with my siblings, which has been referred to as unhealthily codependent before. And it likely is, but after what we've been through, how could we not be.

One hard conversation down, but an even harder one yet to be had.

Chapter 22
Jameson

Having Liv in my apartment feels right on more levels than I can count. She belongs here. She's in my kitchen, my bed, sitting on my couch. Everything about it is perfect. It's probably how she feels having me at her house. Or at least, I hope.

Despite the hangup in the bedroom last night, things have been amazing. The way her eyes light up as we walk around, her clinging to my arm to stay close. She could easily be scared or intimidated, since one block of Manhattan is busier than Juniper Grove on a whole. But she's taking it all in stride and trying to absorb every single thing.

"So. Is this trip also about meeting anybody important to you? I know I haven't been the best girlfriend in not asking about your family"—she swallows sharply on the word—"but it's understandably been something I was trying to avoid."

"Actually, no. I have none to speak of." I rest my ass against the counter and cross my feet at the ankle, a coffee cup in one hand while she sits at the counter and eats the fresh fruit I had delivered for breakfast.

Her face crinkles in confusion as her fork hovers over a piece of honeydew.

"You know I grew up in Connecticut, that I was raised by a single mom. By choice. She was getting older, wanted a child, and my father, whoever he may be, was a literal sperm donor. I've never had much interest in finding out who or where he is because the idea was for him to be anonymous. My mom, though, she was incredible." My eyes drift to the ceiling as a million memories float through my mind.

"What happened to her?" Liv's voice is tiny.

"She passed away a few years ago." I adjust my stance against the counter. "In those last years, I was a terrible son, focusing on my business more than spending time with her. You never know how close the end is."

"How?" Tears well in Liv's eyes.

A throat clear gets rid of the lump starting to build. It's almost more seeing Liv's reaction than how I feel. I loved my mom, very much, but she's been gone five years and I've come to terms with that.

"A heart attack." I take a sip of my coffee to swallow down the emotions. If I had paid better attention, maybe I could have gotten her the help she needed before it was too late. The doctors assured me that wasn't the case, but I can't help but feel it was. Survivor's guilt and all that jazz.

Liv's out of her seat and crosses to me, crashing into my chest and wrapping her arms around my waist as she squeezes herself into me. "I'm so sorry. I had no idea."

"It's okay, Liv. I'm okay with it. I just don't talk about it much."

"Why? Does it still hurt?"

I'm quiet for a minute as I think about her question. "In some ways. But mostly, it's just not something I want to talk about, and most people don't need to know about me. You're the first person in a really long time who I've wanted to share these sides of myself with. You need to know that and understand what that means."

"I do. Probably better than most, since you're the first person I've ever told about my parents." Of course she does. I'm an idiot for even thinking about it. Of all people to understand my hesitance, it's Liv.

Taking her chin in my fingers, I tilt her face up to mine. "I know we have a conversation that's still needed, but I want you to know that I'm in this with you, Liv."

Her body relaxes into mine. "I'm in this too."

My heart slows before picking up speed. She wants to be here as much as I want her here, and while I know family is a problem, maybe there's a way around it. Something I'm not seeing.

Moving to her is a consideration, but she hasn't asked me to, and I won't just assume that's something she wants. It needs to come from her.

Hell, at this point, I'm willing to try long distance and take more jobs up in her area. Maybe I should start looking into the real estate of Juniper Grove.

But would a guy like me thrive in a town like that? Even where I grew up was a bigger town than Juniper Grove. There's not much to do, and if I'm not in my mecca to do my job, is there anything else for me besides Liv?

Mazie hates me, so I doubt she'd let me help with the books and things at the shop, even though it's my area of expertise.

There are so many thoughts and questions and concerns about this future I want to have with Liv that I don't even know how to start to bring it up. But it's doing us no good continuing to ignore the problem as my leaving date looms ever closer.

Chapter 23
Liv

Aphone pings in rapid succession in my general vicinity. We've been at Jameson's for over twenty-four hours, and it's amazing how much his apartment feels like home. How right this all feels. He's in the shower, and I'm enjoying a lazy Saturday afternoon around his apartment before we go explore some more and get dinner. It's an amazing glimpse into what could be life if I'd let it be.

Closing my book, I grab my phone, only to quickly realize it's Jameson's. I've been begging him to change his text ringer for weeks. His response is always that maybe *I* should be the one to change it.

Over my dead body, buddy.

Quickly grabbing it, I flick it open and notice messages from a Charlene. He and I have had an open phone policy since day one, and it's never once bit me in the ass.

Until today.

Hey baby. You have time for a quickie tonight?

Jay. I need an answer.

Am I coming over to do ya tonight or not?

My stomach rolls, all the blood drains to my feet, and my palms moisten, enough for me to drop his phone.

The rage takes over.

I jump to my feet and stomp into his bedroom. The whir of the shower is still going, and knowing Jameson, I have a little while still.

Throwing his closet door wide, I take in all the *very* expensive suits, ties, sport coats, even a few tuxedos. It may be childish, but I've never been accused of acting my age.

Silken material and the softest cotton I've ever felt falls around me as I rip every article of clothing off the hangers, hung in pristine and crisp lines, surely all ironed to contain not a single wrinkle.

I wonder if there are scissors anywhere. A few sliced coats, cut ties, and shirts missing sleeves should do that trick.

"That lying, motherfucking bast—"

"I'm what now?"

Oh fuck.

Chapter 24
Jameson

The sound of hangers clanging together is what greets me when I get out of the shower. Not my girl, not a fresh cup of coffee, none of the sweet things she's said or done in the past.

With a heavy sigh, I pull on a pair of pants and walk quietly toward the closet.

My eyes widen as I take in the scene. Liv, hair wild and breathing heavily, tearing down *almost* every article of clothing I own. They litter the floor around her in giant piles.

When she starts mumbling to herself, I interrupt before she gets the word "bastard" out.

"I'm what now?" I raise one eyebrow, as though to challenge her to finish the thought.

With one giant step, she's in front of me, shoving her hands against my chest so hard I actually move back a step.

"What the fuck, Liv?"

Her finger is right in my face and fury rips through her. I have no idea why, since I'm the one who has a right to be angry with the state my closet is in.

"What the fuck is right, Jameson. Am I just some game to you? Some fun, small-town ass?"

My brows furrow. "What are you talking about?"

"Some girl named *Charlene* messaged you and asked for a quickie tonight."

Laughter takes over, and my head tips back as a hand clutches my chest.

But it's quickly over when Liv pushes me again. "This isn't funny, Jameson!"

My head snaps back up to face her. "It's hilarious, actually."

This time, when she tries to push me again, I catch her and wrap my arms tightly around her. "Let me go! You bring me here and can't even tell your city whore that we've been together? You tell me you love me and still have *her* waiting in the wings for you for when you return? Or for a quick weekend trip here and there?"

"Would you be quiet and let me explain, please? Because I promise you'll laugh when you finally understand."

"Doubtful."

"Liv. I *do* love you. And *only* you—"

"You don't need to love somebody to fuck them."

"Shh. Listen to me. Charlene is my *cleaning lady*. I work late hours, so she comes at night or on weekends because I don't like people being in my apartment when I'm not around. She's at least fifty, smokes a pack a day, and is definitely not at all my type. She's asking about a 'quickie' because she doesn't always have time to do a full, deep clean."

My voice is calm and level, trying to make her understand without it being confrontational.

"Wait. What?" And just like that, all the steam she had built up inside her gushes out, and she deflates in my arms.

"It's only you, baby. Nobody else."

"Your cleaning lady."

"Yes. My cleaning lady." I raise my hand to show my full honesty.

A sheepish grin takes over and her cheeks turn pink. "I'll, um, I'll help you clean up the mess."

"You bet your fine ass you will."

"Be thankful you got here before I found a pair of scissors." She tips up on her toes to press a kiss against my cheek and pats my chest as horror rips through me. She was going to cut up my clothes? My *very* expensive clothes?

A shudder wracks through my body. Seth has always called her a firecracker. He's not wrong. But I never thought she'd go for the suits. She knows they're important to me. A sign that I've made something of myself and worked hard at my job. She likes to make fun of me for them, but she knows I need them. They're part of me, like her torn jeans are part of her.

She was really mad, going right for where she knew it would hurt. But how could she possibly think that I'd be using her to cheat? Or that I'd cheat on her? I guess we never really had a conversation about that aspect. We shared that we were single, but never had an exclusivity discussion. I assumed since I was with her twenty-four-seven, she got the message.

Maybe I shouldn't have assumed. I'm living in her home, her town, so I know her moves and friends and family. But she doesn't know what my life is like here. It makes sense for her to jump to that conclusion with the messages she saw.

For all she knows, I'm used to having a girl around down here. But I don't. And while I told her, and I wish she understood that, a little unsureness is understandable.

I'll have to make it even more clear to her that my intentions are on her and her alone. As though anybody else could even compare. Silly girl.

Chapter 25
Liv

Part of me feels like an idiot for assuming his cleaning lady was a hookup. The other part of me is mad at him for not telling me about her in the first place. How hard is it to mention that you have a cleaning lady who may swing by while we're around?

But he's an attractive man who lives on his own and works long hours. A consistent hookup isn't the craziest idea.

Though it's really not Jameson's style. I realize that now.

We put away all his suits and garments in silence. A few gasps from Jameson leave his chest as he realizes which articles landed on the floor. I've been making fun of him for being a suit from day one, but I never realized how many he had. Or how extensive. His closet space nearly doubles my own and one of his suits is worth at least three of my more expensive outfits. I'm pretty sure the whole closet is worth more than my house.

None of it helps me feel better, though. If anything, I feel worse, as it's a stark reminder of how truly different we are. Where he's suits and designer clothes, I'm ripped jeans and t-shirts. He's corporate, and I'm front end.

He's big city, and I'm small-town.

We're very different and it's hard to ignore. While it didn't bother me before, and these are things I've known since day one, the fact that his departure is looming over us like a dark cloud is something that's making this feeling worse.

Once the last suit is hanging neatly in its place, Jameson throws his arm around my shoulder and pulls me into his side, kissing the top of my head.

"Thanks for not truly destroying anything."

"You stopped me just in time." A nervous smile pulls up the corners of my lips. I want to tease him, but somehow, I just can't seem to get it in me right now.

"What are you in the mood for, for dinner tonight?"

"Hmm. I don't know. There are so many choices."

"Literally anything you want within a few minutes. We did Italian last night. Let's do something different. How about Indian?"

"I've never had it before."

His eyebrows go high. "Never?"

I shake my head. "Nope. Nowhere in Juniper Grove, and it wasn't something I was ever brave enough to try when I was in Pineville City."

"Well, there we go then. I'll take you to my favorite spot and you can try some delicious food. Naan is a must, as is basmati rice, and you'll probably love tandoori chicken."

I look up at him with wide eyes. It all sounds like it could be delicious, and I know he'd never steer me wrong. "Is it spicy?"

"Some things can be, but I'll let help you figure out what to order." The fact that he knows my dislike of spicy foods warms straight through my heart. All these tiny things make facing the reality of our temporary status that much harder.

We get ready without another mention of the situation in the closet, and I'm thankful he's choosing to ignore my mini meltdown. He did say that if I'm okay with it, he'd like Charlene to stop by tonight, but if I'm not, that it's alright and he can have her come next time.

But next time is when he's done working with Seth and he's back home.

I said she can come tonight. Partially because I feel like a fool, and partially to be sure she's as explained.

Leaving the apartment, we walk around the city. Everything is still awe inspiring. I can't help but be wowed by my surroundings; the tall buildings, the hundreds of people, the bustle of everything zipping around me and moving like it's a living organism.

I cling to Jameson, not just because of the busyness of the street, but so I don't get lost. "It's all so amazing. Everything is just right outside your door."

Literally. We've passed shopping, a dozen eateries of different kinds, hot dog and pretzel vendors, which both smell amazing.

"The big city, babe. You'd really love it here."

A tight smile pulls at my cheeks. I know I'd love it, and I want it so badly, but my siblings mean more to me than my dreams. I can't be hours away from them. I just can't.

Dinner's delicious, and I send Alina a quick text letting her know I have found a new favorite food. She seems surprised but assures me she'll learn how to cook it so we can all try it.

The chicken is moist and delicious, seasoned delightfully with a little tang and punch, but not too spicy. The rice has a bit of an earthy flavor to it in comparison to what you'd get at a Chinese restaurant. And the naan, well, I'm pretty sure this bread is from heaven. It's pillowy and soft and luxurious in my mouth.

The whole dinner is amazing.

Being with Jameson has opened my life and mind to so many new things; it's almost staggering how little I feel like I knew and had experienced before. I know I'm still young, but there are some things that I feel I should have done by now.

I'm glad I'm sharing these moments with him. That he's getting some of these firsts with me.

After dinner, we walk arm in arm around the block a few times. "Any shops you want to stop in, just let me know."I nod but am too stunned to say anything. It never gets old. The brightness, the noise. Once you're inside, you can almost forget it exists because you can't see it, can't hear it. But the second you're back out in it, it's in your face again.

"I love it, Jameson. Really. Thank you for bringing me here."

He stops in the middle of the sidewalk and hooks his fingers through mine, putting them at the base of my spine and pulling my body against his. "You're welcome. I wanted you to experience it and I wanted to be the one you did that with."

Squeezing his fingers, I push up on my toes and press my lips to his. "I love you."

"I love you too."

I loop my arm through his and cling to his side as we continue our journey around the block before heading back to his apartment.

I can see us doing this day in and day out. Going for dinner and walking the block before heading back upstairs. Waking and ordering breakfast from the shop downstairs.

The only problem with everything is how far away it is from Juniper Grove.

Chapter 26

Jameson

I know Liv says she can't live in the city, and it's not exactly that I'm trying to convince her that she can, or even should. But I am showing her the best time I possibly can.

The never-ceasing smile on her face tells me I'm doing a good job. Every so often, she'll tug at my hand, pull me toward something, or grab my arm and squeal. Our fingers have been intertwined since we left the apartment.

Having her so close, not needing to share her attention, is more than I could have hoped for and absolutely something I wish could happen every single day.

When the job is done, in just three short weeks, I have nothing keeping me in Juniper Grove except for her, and while I love her tremendously, that's not really enough of a reason for me to quit my job and move. Is it?

I've considered doing it from there. It's not impossible, but also not favorable. I do a ton of work in the city alone. The rest of the time? I'm traveling. I can't leave her for all that time, going from one job to the next, and I doubt she'd come with me for every single trip.

Leaning against my side, her hand comfortably in mine as she snacks on her pretzel, a smile pulls at my lips as I look down at her. I can tell she's content and vaguely see her upturned lips. Her feet are shuffling, and our steps have slowed considerably since this morning.

"You tired, Sweetheart?"

"A little."

"It's a big new world for you." So far, we've kept pretty close to home, but today's the last day and I wanted to show her some new sights.

"So much to see and do; I still feel like we've barely scratched the surface."

"This doesn't have to be your only trip here, Liv." Hopefully, it won't be. Not even close.

"I can't live here, Jameson." There's such finality to her voice, but I wonder if she's even considered it.

"I'm not saying you should. I mean, I do think you should, but that's not what I'm suggesting. Maybe we can do long distance. You can come visit, and I'll visit you."

"What about when you have to travel?"

The air rushes from my lungs. I've barely been able to eat all day just thinking about it.

"I don't know, Liv." I stop and turn toward her, cupping her face with my hands. "All I know is that I have to be with you. There's no other option than that."

Her eyes flutter closed, and a shimmer graces her eyelashes. Swiping my thumbs across them, I pull her against me before the tears can fall.

"Please don't cry, baby. I can't stand it." The thought alone tears my insides apart, each section wanting to go a different way.

"What are we going to do, Jay? I didn't want this. I didn't plan for this. Ever."

"You know I feel the same way, Liv. I've been married to my job since I started seven years ago, and I never regretted that. Until I met you. I had no plans of anything between us."

Standing in the middle of the sidewalk in downtown Manhattan has never seemed like something I would do, yet here I am, holding the woman I love as people mill around us. They move like a stream and we're a mere rock in the way.

"Maybe you should have made less delicious coffee."

"Maybe you shouldn't have been an asshole who I needed to prove wrong."

"Well, that part is impossible."

She shakes with a laugh, but it quickly turns into sobs, and her whole body rattles. Her pretzel drops to the ground as she twists her fingers into the front of my shirt.

I wrap my arms around her upper half, enclosing her head so she's both shielded from onlookers and her senses are only overwhelmed with me.

My jaw clamps together, and I have to fight the urge to ball my hands into fists. This is all my fault. I'm such a fucking idiot. What did I think was going to happen falling in love with a small-town girl with a history such as hers? It's not just my heart involved, my life to ruin. It's hers too.

Trailing my lips along the top of her head, I take a deep inhale, filling my nose and lungs with her jasmine scent.

"Let's go home, have some dinner." She's already shaking her head. "Yes, Liv. We're going to go back to my apartment, order whatever you want for dinner, and I'm going to give you a foot massage because I'm sure your feet are killing you walking around in those things." I told her wearing heels was a terrible idea for walking around the city. "And then I'm going to hold you. For hours and hours." Though we're here for the weekend, we chose a long one and took through Monday, with plans to leave right after breakfast tomorrow so we can both get at least a half day of work in.

She sniffles a few times, not really giving me more than that. "Okay."

I keep her pressed to my side as we walk the several blocks back to my apartment.

Once we get back upstairs, she immediately kicks her heels off and pads over to the couch, flopping down onto it. I put her shopping bags by the door and lock it behind me, joining her on the sofa.

Immediately, I take her left foot in my hands and start rubbing. Her head dips back against the couch with a moan that I wish was for other reasons, but I love my ability to bring any kind of pleasure to this woman and the sounds she makes.

Working my thumbs into the sole of her foot, flexing and kneading the muscles, she melts beneath me.

"God, Jameson. Why does everything you do to my body have to be so damn incredible?"

A smirk pulls up one side of my mouth, but I don't stop working her foot. When I lean down and take the other, she collapses back into the couch and her eyes flutter shut. Her moans lessen as I keep massaging her foot and her breaths even out.

I laugh to myself as I lay her legs flat on the couch and tuck her in, kissing her forehead. I knew today had to be exhausting for her. Not just because of the shoes but from how much walking we did. It's a lot if you're not used to it.

She's so peaceful, I hate to wake her, but my stomach is grumbling. I didn't snack on the street food quite as much as she did, though she didn't finish her pretzel.

As much as I'd love to curl up and join her, I decide ordering food is best. Thankfully, I know what she likes and would want to eat, so I order from my favorite Japanese restaurant and sit next to her on the couch while I read the newspaper and wait for food to be delivered.

I don't let myself dwell on how normal it all feels, instead focusing on the news and what's going on in the world. It's far bleaker, but that may be for the best, as the future between Liv and myself remains an unknown.

Chapter 27
Liv

The second Jameson's tongue touches my soaking pussy, my fingers dive into his hair, tugging and tousling it. He'll complain because he has to go back to work, but what does he expect from me when he's licking me so good it's almost otherworldly.

He keeps going, licking and sucking and swirling while holding me tightly so I can't move while I buck and writhe. It's the only time that I hate how strong he is. Normally, his strong grip on me is something I adore, something that makes me feel safe for the first time in years. But right now, I need to *move*.

Weeks ago, he told me he does it because it makes me come faster. And while I wanted to disagree, he's right. That familiar building of delicious pressure takes over, and I buck a few more times, my head tilting back as I shudder and come against his mouth with a loud scream, yanking at his roots.

With a few kisses to the inside of my thighs, he moves his body up over me. He presses his forehead against mine, saying quietly, "You're the most amazing woman in this whole fucking world, Liv." And then he slowly eases into me, and we both suck in the air mingling between us.

He rocks his hips, slowly at first, before picking up momentum.

I have never known a love like Jameson's. And I would be okay to never know another love again.

That thought scares the shit out of me, in more ways than one. The least of which is that this has a time limit. His job here is almost done, and after that? Well, after that is still unknown. He lives in the city, I live here. The two locations are hours apart, and my work at the café doesn't allow for frequent long, luxurious weekends or weeks away.

I broke my cardinal rule of not falling for somebody who I know is going to break my heart. It's why I haven't had a relationship in a long time. Because the chance for heartbreak always exists.

Yet with Jameson, it's all been worth it. The ache already exists in my heart, I can feel it deep in my bones, ready to take over my entire being, my entire soul. It's just a matter of time.

"Hey, gorgeous. Where'd you go? I'm doing some of my best work here and your mind is clearly off in another world."

"Sorry. Trust me, my body is still here."

"Yeah, I can fucking tell, but I want your mind too, Liv."

Instead of answering, I clasp my hand behind his neck and pull his face to mine, forcing my tongue to meet his and kissing him deeply before nibbling at his lower lip. "Fuck me, Jay. The way only you can."

"God, Liv, why are you so incredible?" I know he wanted to fall for me less than I wanted to fall for him. We're a match made in heaven, in a hellish situation.

He thrusts into me hard and fast, my body shifting on the bed with the motions. When I texted him asking for a quickie instead of lunch, I thought he'd say no. Seems he's trying to get in as much extra time as I am.

"You take my cock so good, baby." He laces our fingers together, resting his forearms on mine.

I try to answer, but it comes out more like some broken syllables. My nails dig into his shoulders as he continues to thrust hard and fast into me. "Jay." His name falls from my lips as I tighten around him.

A few more thrusts and he falls against me with a groan, his forehead dipping to my shoulder.

He kisses his way to my ear and gives the lobe a nibble before he rolls to his side.

"Good call on the midday romp. I was not at all expecting it."

"Romp?" I laugh at his choice of words.

"What else do you want me to call it?"

"A solid fucking."

"Fine. Nice call on the midday solid fucking." He rolls his eyes, and I snuggle into his chest. I'm going to miss this.

"You know. This doesn't have to end, Liv." Clearly, his mind is in exactly the same place as mine.

My whole body tightens, because now, after *that* is not the time to be having this conversation.

"And do what, Jameson? Leave my family? I told you I won't do that."

"Have you ever considered me moving here? You've never once brought it up. Would you not want me to live with you? I basically do anyway."

"I can't ask you to give up your life for me. And you would be. You're not a small-town guy, Jameson. You're a city boy, basically born and raised. This life isn't for you, and you'd resent me for it in a matter of months." It'd be impossible not to. Especially now that I've seen all he'd be giving up.

"You don't know that."

I push out of bed and rip my clothes back on. "I do. I'm not having this conversation right now. Let's go get lunch."

He's out of bed just as fast and getting back into his suit. Another stark reminder of what he'd be giving up. He sticks out like a sore thumb in this town.

"We can't keep ignoring the elephant in the room, Liv." He grabs my bicep and spins me toward him. "We have to talk about this."

But I shrug him off. "Not right now we don't."

I stomp out of my room and down the hall toward the front door. He won't talk to me about it at work, so that's exactly where I'm going.

He's just walking into the hallway as I'm tugging my shoes on, prepared to leave.

"Really? You're going to just walk out while we're in the middle of a conversation."

"We're not in the middle of anything, number one. And number two, you always say I'm a child anyway. So why not act like one?"

"Liv, this is beneath you and you know it."

I do. Him calling me on it doesn't change that I know how completely childish I'm being. But I just can't bear to think of where this conversation is going to go, and I'm not in the mood to be devastated right now.

"I'm going back to work. I'll see you later." I'm out the door before he has a chance to answer and walking through the door to Three Sticks in a matter of minutes.

Thankfully, I didn't hit the one red light on my way in.

But he must have left just after me, because before I can even say "hi" to Alina, he's jumping out of his car and stalking through the front door as he buttons his sport coat.

This is all too much. My lungs are constricting, my palms are sweaty. He's trying to have the conversation where I have to break my own heart.

And I just can't bear to do that.

Chapter 28
Jamson

“I can’t talk to you right now.” Holding up her hand and shaking her head, Liv storms off, through the swinging door into the kitchen. No man’s land, as I’ve come to know it. We’ve been at this for a few months, telling each other we love each other every day for most of that time. And yet, I’ve never made it through that damn door.

“Jay, can I give you some advice?” Alina’s soft voice pulls my attention from the blackness protecting Liv.

“Sure.”

Her caramel eyes sparkle as her mouth quirks up at the corners. “Liv is…strong-willed. You know that. She’s never going to leave us, Jameson. Once Liv sets her mind to something, that’s it, the decision is made and there’s no changing that. Not for anybody or anything. Liv’s decided to stay *here* with *us*. It’s not necessarily the choice we’d all make for her, but it’s the one she’s made for herself, and that’s all any of us need to know.”

“I’m not trying to get her to leave, Alina.” It’s the truth. I’m not trying to convince her to do anything right now except talk to me. Go over the options. Together, we can surely figure something out.

"What it seems like you need to decide is if you're staying in this town or not. But let me say one thing. Be careful. Liv's been through a lot, we all have. She's been with her fair share of men."

I stiffen at her words. I'm not an idiot. I know Liv had experience before me, but that doesn't mean I have to like it.

"I have *never* seen her as comfortable with another man as she is with you. The way she leans into you, the way she smiles when you're around. It's like she seeks you out in any room, gravitates toward you. It's honestly kind of incredible, and it's how I know her feelings are real. That she will be absolutely *crushed* if things don't work out. And Liv being Liv, she'll probably try to act first. Protect herself from the damage by pushing you away. If she is what you want, if this"—she holds her arms out around her—"could be enough for you, then stand strong. Otherwise, don't push back."

"Alina!" The holler comes from the kitchen, and I know my time is limited.

"Coming, Maze," she shouts in return, but doesn't take her eyes off me. "Think about what I said. Okay?"

"Thanks, Alina." I'm pretty sure she's the only one in this family who even sort of likes me, aside from Liv, of course.

And I do think about what she said, all damn day. Seth can barely grab my attention. I'm utterly worthless at my job today, and that has never happened.

Yet when I leave at five, I'm still no closer to a decision than I was this morning. I love Liv, with every fiber of my being. But to live here? I don't know if I can do that. City living is in my bones.

When I get to Liv's home, it seems the decision has been made for me. My clothes litter the lawn, with even more are coming.

Storming up the lawn, I narrowly miss a Hugo Boss suit being chucked onto the pile. "What the fuck are you doing?"

"Taking out the trash."

"I see, so is it my clothes that are trash or me?" My hands are planted firmly on my hips inside my now open suit jacket. I run a palm over my mouth as I assess the damage. Thousands of dollars in clothes and shoes. And it rained today. So at least the bottom layers are soaked. I'm sure she made sure the truly expensive brands were the first to go.

"Guess they're the same thing, right?"

Walking up the stairs to the front porch, I take her upper arms in my hands and tug her toward me. Fire rages in her violet eyes.

"What's going on, Liv? You're making a scene."

"Why would you care what the neighbors think? You won't be around anyway." She forcefully pushes out of my grasp.

"I haven't decided that yet."

Turning away, she runs her fingertips along her scalp and tugs at her roots. I know I'm in for a lashing before she even looks back to me. "It shouldn't be a hard decision, Jameson! Do you love me? Do you care for me at all?" There it is. The words she hasn't once uttered but yet I was supposed to decipher. She wants me to stay, because it means I truly love her. And if I don't stay, I must not love her.

"Of course I do! You know I do. It's not that simple, Olivia. I have a *career*, a successful one. I've made a name for myself in my industry. That means something." It's the biggest factor that's making me not just throw it all away and move here.

"And I don't? I don't mean anything?"

"You mean everything, Liv."

"Clearly not enough if you're leaving me." Her voice breaks and her eyes flood.

"Olivia." I reach out for her, but she pulls away.

"Go. Just leave, Jameson. You're going to anyway." This is not the same girl I left at the café a few hours ago. Somebody has been whispering in her ear. And I have a good idea who that might be.

"No, I'm not leaving without a discussion. I wanted to talk about this, about the implications of trying to make it work, of being together." I've been trying and trying, hoping to avoid some sort of situation like this.

"I don't want to do that. Just leave." She waves her hand in the direction of the driveway, shooing me away, like I'll just leave that simply.

"You can't just tell me to leave."

"All your shit on my front lawn says otherwise." Her violet eyes meet mine with a fiery passion. She's hurt and she's angry and she's refusing to hear reason.

"Baby, please. Talk to me. Let me come inside. Let's *talk* about this." I'm at the point of pleading. Because I can't just go. That's not possible anymore.

"Don't *baby* me. Just leave. Please, Jameson. Make this easier on the both of us and just *go*." I see the second her heart breaks, and all I want is to pull her into my arms and hold her and hug her and kiss her. But Alina's words run through my mind, and I know there's no going back. Not right now, at least.

Gathering my things from the lawn, I toss them into the bags, also out on the grass, and throw everything into the car. I'll sort through it later, tomorrow, whenever.

I still have a few days left with Seth, so with one last look at Liv, her arms wrapped tight around her middle and refusing to even glance in my direction, I drive over to the motel I first stayed in.

I know the drill from here. I'm basically going back to the way it was when I started. Except I'll be finding a new coffee shop.

Dragging my feet, I open the door to the dusty room and flop onto the bed. I'm utterly exhausted and broken.

Is my career more important than Liv? Maybe it shouldn't be. But we've only known each other for a few months. Sure, this is the strongest I have ever felt toward another human, but is that enough to give up my career? I've worked hard to cultivate it all, to build my name. Being in a relationship, potential marriage, was never in my mind, never in my plans.

And if I stay, that's what it says, isn't it? That I want to get married to Liv? Why would I give up everything else if I didn't?

The ceiling starts to swirl, just like the thoughts in my head. The fact that I just lost Liv hasn't even settled in yet, and I know it's going to be completely incapacitating when it does.

I'm glad these next few days with Seth are simple and straight forward. I'm sure if it required more brain power, something, then it'd be a problem.

The longer I lie here, the less things feel right or like I can leave them as they are. How am I supposed to just disappear? Be in the same town as her, knowing she's not far away, and just pretend she doesn't exist?

It's not possible.

I'm on my feet and out the door before I have a game plan, quickly pulling up in front of her house. I pound the front door with so much force, I'm afraid I might knock it down or scare her. It's presumptuous to use my key, which I need to leave this time. I've already taken it off the keyring.

Her eyes are red-rimmed and puffy when she pulls open the door.

"Olivia, please, talk to me. We can work this out." We have to.

"We can't, Jameson. There's nothing to work out. We never should have been anything, never should have given in to those desires." It's something I've thought over too. What if we never gave in that night?

But then everything we would have experienced together would have been for nothing and that can't be either.

"You can't mean that. Despite what's happening now, you can't mean that. Everything we've done, what we've become?"

"And what have we become, Jameson? Two people fighting on my front lawn, again."

"Two people who love each other, Liv. Two people who need to figure out how to continue this relationship that we both want." Only none of this is a want, it's a deep need, something that has to be done. I can't imagine life without Liv.

"We don't both want it anymore, Jameson." There's a tired resoluteness to her voice.

"I do."

"I don't."

"You don't mean that. I know you can't possibly mean that." She can't. I won't be able to handle it if she does.

"I have to. You're *leaving*, Jameson. I can't be with somebody who isn't *here* with me." She points to the ground beneath her, like this location is all that matters.

"It's one of the things we need to discuss."

She growls and runs her hands through her hair. "Dammit, no, it's not. Don't drag this out. Just go. Please, just leave."

"Liv, baby, please. Don't send me away." My hands clasp in front of me. I'm begging. Truly begging, because she can't just end things. We were doing so well. We just had sex a few hours ago. How did we get to this point in just a matter of hours?

"Leave. Don't come back. I can't...I won't be able to handle it if you come back. I won't be able to turn you away again."

"Don't turn me away *now*. Come on, let's talk about thi—"

"She said to leave, Jameson." Mazie stands, tall and proud for her five-foot-two frame, at the top of the porch stairs, her arms crossed tight against her chest. The light shining out from the house behind her gives her an illumination that darkens her features and makes her truly terrifying.

Shifting my eyes back to my main focus, I find her curled in on herself, those arms wrapped around her middle again. All I want is to hold her, comfort her. But just standing here, I'm causing her pain.

Unable to help myself, I take a step forward. When Liv takes a step backward, my heart all but stops. "Liv, hear me. If I get in that car and drive away, that's it. I'm done with Seth. I'm packed and ready to go." Mostly I just didn't have it in me to take the clothes from the car, even though I planned to stay a few more days. Now? I'm not sure I can. Everything with Seth would be fine if I took off this very second. "If I leave, it's really over. I know it's complicated and messy but, baby, I'd marry you tomorrow and figure out how to make it work. Because all I want is *you*."

Her eyes lift to meet mine and they're filled with fire and pain. "And your job. Don't forget that's the hold up here, Jay."

"I need to make money, Liv! I can't just burn it all to the ground either."

"Well, then we are where we are. Go, Jameson. There's nothing here for you anymore." Her tone is defeated, and I can tell she's truly given up. But there's one last thing I'm holding on to.

"If that's what you really want." There's hesitation to my statement. Because Liv hasn't really said it's what she wants. I have a strong feeling that a lot of this is coming from the woman standing behind her.

"She's said it a dozen times, Jameson. You're not getting your way here. You were never good enough for her, never going to do more than use her and drop her. You knew it when you started, and now we all do. Now leave." Mazie has stepped down from the porch to wrap her arms around Liv. She's taller than Mazie, by a good two inches, but Mazie stands larger than life with her strength, and Liv turns into her.

I can't tear my eyes from her as I back away toward the car. Her shoulders are shaking and I'm sure I hear a sob.

Getting in the car and driving away is the hardest thing I've ever had to do, and yet somehow, I manage to put my foot to the pedal and drive away, leaving Liv in my rearview mirror.

By the time I reach the highway, my whole body aches. Her scent lingers in the car, on my skin, my clothes. It's everywhere. I both want to be rid of it and find a way to keep it forever.

I always put the towns behind me when I finish the jobs. A spot on a map, a destination I can say I've visited. This one is so much more.

This one is where I left my heart.

Chapter 29
Liv

"What did I do? What did I *do?*" Frantically, I pace the living room, my hands roped into my hair.

"Nothing that can't be undone, Liv." Alina reaches toward me with her calm demeanor, but I turn on her like a rabid animal.

"He left, Alina! How can that be undone?"

"Go to him."

"You want me to go to his apartment, uninvited, after throwing all of his belongings out of my house and onto the lawn, which was soaking wet, might I add, and, what? Beg for his forgiveness? Beg for him to love me?"

"He *does* love you, Olivia. You know that."

"No, no, he did. I know that he *did*. But after that, and after what she said to him, he can't possibly anymore." I point my finger, angrily and accusatory at my oldest sister as the reality of what I just did sets in.

"Me? What did I do?" Mazie's hand flies to her chest.

"Why did I listen? Why did I let you sway my judgment?" My eyes are wide and wild, my fingers knotting in my hair. My pulse is the fastest I've ever felt it, and I can't stop moving. Because if I stop then all the pieces fall into place.

"Eli, we need you at Liv's. She's having a crisis. It's all hands on deck." I hadn't even noticed that Mazie pulled out her phone.

"Of course I'm having a crisis! You chased away the love of my life!" Silence blankets the room at my exclamation. It's not news, not really. They all knew it. But it's the first time I've vocalized it.

Ten minutes later, Eli walks through the front door and into a war.

"You never liked him, Mazie! You made that fact well known. You never even gave him a chance. You were completely unwilling to see what I saw in him. Hell, not even that, you didn't accept the fact that he made me *happy*." Anger claws at my chest like a feral animal trying to escape.

"That's ridiculous. I didn't trust him, Liv. I knew he was going to do what he did."

"And what's that, Mazie, love me? Did he love me too much?" I hold my hands out to the side. My voice raises with each word.

"He left, Liv!"

"You chased him away!" I point an accusatory finger at her. It's her fault. Everything is always Mazie's fault.

"If he loved you enough, he would have stayed."

I'm shaking my head before she's done, because I know it's not true. I know Jameson loves me, *loved* me, more than anything. There were details we had to work out, things we had to discuss. We're from two different places, and that's a normal conversation for people who live in different locations to have. And I refused to entertain it. I let Mazie and her negativity plant seeds of doubt in my mind. And they blossomed into full blown flowers. The first hint of him leaving, and I threw it all away without a second thought.

"You're not happy, Mazie, and that means nobody else can be either. You're the oldest, you want to be the first to fall in love, get married, live happily ever after, and because you're not, none of us can be."

"That's ridiculous, Liv. He was no good—"

"Stop. You need to leave. I love you, Mazie, you're my sister, but I can't look at you right now. Please go."

She opens her mouth to talk, but my other siblings intervene. In all the shouting, I'd forgotten they were even here. Alina wraps her arm around my shoulder and leads me to the kitchen, while Eli does the same to Mazie and leads her out the front door and into the night.

"He's gone, Leen. He's really gone." The dam breaks, and I cover my face as I lean into her shoulder.

"Shh, I know, Sibby. I know." She rocks me from side to side. She doesn't try to calm me, doesn't give any reassuring words. Probably because she knows there are none to be had right now.

As the tears stop flowing and the body rattling tremors cease, I hear voices outside the front door. I know who it is without having to look.

Stomping my way to the door, I'm about to throw it open and tell Mazie and Eli to get the hell off my porch, when I hear Mazie's pained voice. It's the one she uses when she feels guilty or knows she's done something to upset us.

"Am I really like that, Eli? Am I not allowing room for anybody's happiness until I find my own?"

"I can't answer that for you, Maze. But what I can tell you is that Liv was right about one thing. You *never* gave Jameson a chance. You never even tried to."

I should feel bad about eavesdropping, but I can't get myself to feel anything more than the ache in my chest.

"He's a big-city guy. What could he want with a girl like Liv aside from using her and disposing of her? Getting some small-town tail and then leaving again?"

"You don't give either of them enough credit, Mae. How you don't see the love those two have for each other is beyond me. It's clear as day. And what you're not looking at are all the things he can give her that we can't. He can give her that city life she wants but refuses, Mazie. Something we can't, something she won't take while with us."

Eli's calming voice is working its effects right through the door as my body stops shaking, and I twirl a curl, leaning my back against the wall and my forehead against the cool door.

"She won't leave us, that's her choice."

"No, she won't. But he can still give it to her. He can take her away on weekends, whisk her off to Paris on a whim. Things we can't do for her, things she won't do for herself."

"How do you see that? All I see is the pain that he could cause her." There's a sorrowness to her tone and I want to feel sorry for Mazie. But she does this to herself; she dug this hole.

"I keep my eyes open, Mae. That's all it is. Dad taught me to be overtly aware of you three, of the men in your lives, and he swore there would be multiple. He was right about that. So that's what I try to do. It took me a bit, but I warmed up to Jameson. Because I saw those things, and I realized all he can give her. And, really, I think Dad would have liked him. I think he would have liked them together."

My heart skips a beat and my eyes flutter at his last sentence. None of us will ever get our father's seal of approval on the man we plan to marry, and we'll never walk down the aisle on his arm to be handed off. But this little tidbit? This means more to me than any of them can ever know.

"Mom would have talked about how attractive he is." I can't help but giggle. It's definitely something Mom would have commented on.

"How do I fix this, Eli? How do I make this right?"

"Honestly? I don't know, Mazie. He's gone, and it seems too late. I think at this point, all you can do is try to repair your relationship with Olivia. Because it's surely damaged from this."

Of the four of us, the girls are together far more often than we are with Eli. But somehow, he's the glue. He keeps us all together, he sees everything, he understands what isn't voiced. How, I don't know. But I think he stole a little of Mom and Dad's magic before they passed.

"Fuck. How did I let it come to this?"

"We all make mistakes, Mazie. Don't hold it against yourself too much."

"She's going to hate me forever now." I watch out the small window at the top of the door as Mazie drops her head into her hands. I should walk away. I know I should. But I can't.

"Forever? No. A long time? Entirely possible. But just hang in. Keep at it. Don't let her push you away, and she'll definitely try."

"Any fast tips for me?" I know she's asking because of the bond Eli and I have. It's stronger than what I have with Mazie. Probably because all Mazie's ever done is mother me when sometimes I needed a sister.

"Sorry, Mae, you have to do this one on your own."

"Ugh, I just always feel so distant from her! You two, and she and Alina, have such strong bonds, and she and I just...don't."

"You're always so hard on her."

"Because she's young and irresponsible!"

My hand is resting on the doorknob, about to twist and yank the door open, when Eli takes care of things.

"Mazie, have you *seen* Olivia lately? She may have hot pink streaks in her hair, but she is far from irresponsible. Yes, she is only twenty-three, but she owns and runs one third of a very successful café. She's there almost all day, every single day, even while Jameson was around. I mean, shit, Mazie, she bought a fucking house." He holds his hands out and turns from side to side. When he's facing the door, our eyes meet and he softens, shooting me a quick wink before turning back to Mazie.

My big brother. A lot of girls will say their older brother is their hero, but mine really is. He always comes to my rescue, any time of day or night. He's the one sibling who has a close bond with all three of us.

"I think for now the best you can do is give her a little space. Starting now. I can take you home if you don't want to drive."

"How much time? She's my sister, Eli. I know we're not super close, but I love her."

"I know. Let her come to you. She will."

"How do you know?"

Turning his head around, he looks at me again. He must see something that I'm not aware of because his lips turn up into a smile before he answers her. "I just do."

Chapter 30

Jameson

Being back at my apartment without Liv doesn't feel right. She was here for one weekend and yet it changed the course of everything for me.

It doesn't help that there's no work for me to focus on except finishing out the last bits of paperwork for Seth.

I chose to leave instead of extending my stay a few days. I wasn't needed there, and it was too much for me to think about staying in town. It was too small; I'd surely have run into Liv.

I've been home for three weeks and everything still reminds me of her. I can't go to any of my favorite restaurants because I took her to them. The scent of jasmine still lingers in the air, though Charlene has been by a few times.

She's here now, the drone of the vacuum going in the other room while I sit on the couch with my laptop open on my lap.

"Sugar. What's got you down?" I was so focused on the email for jobs in front of me that I didn't even hear the vacuum shut off. "And hey, where's that pretty lady of yours?"

"We, uh, we broke up." I use the trackpad to move the next email without lifting my gaze. I don't want to get into it, least of all with Charlene. It's part of why I left without really talking to Seth. He'd ask questions and I'd have to come up with answers I don't have.

"What? You two kids were so happy last time you were here." I lift my gaze and frown as she sits on the end of the couch. While I don't mind her chatting or sitting, this is the last thing I want to do right now.

"Things just reached their end. She's from a small town, I'm from here. It never would have worked out." It's the party line I keep telling myself in the dark and quiet hours of the night when my longing for Liv reaches its peak.

"You two seemed like you were going to take on the world together. Shame. If there's no happy ending for a couple like you, then I have no idea what hope there is for the rest of us." She pats her knees and stands, wheeling the vacuum toward the door. "I'm done for the day, darling. I'll let you know my schedule for next time."

"Thank you, Charlene." I barely lift my gaze to look at her, because she's reopened wounds that had started to scab over.

My head falls back to the top of the couch with the click of the door.

I was hoping the longer I was away the more this feeling of longing and loss would go away, but it hasn't so far. And nothing seems to bring it close to vacating my body.

The thought of picking up the phone and calling her plagues my thoughts. Driving up to see her haunts my dreams. But none of that is something I feel like I can actually do. I don't know that any of it will be well-received and I can't face more of her turning me away. Once was enough to last a lifetime.

So instead, I sit here in misery, wanting nothing more than the girl who turned my world on its head.

She hasn't called and neither have I. What does one say after being kicked to the curb, begging to be taken back, and is still turned away?

Nothing.

Which is why I left and never looked back. Though my mind wanders back to those wonderful days and nights with Liv, all they'll be now are memories.

Chapter 31
Liv

It's been almost ten weeks since I last saw Jameson, and not a second has gotten any easier or less painful. I still miss him just as much as day one.

Mazie and I barely talk to one another. She tries, but then the ache of missing Jameson resurfaces and it's back to the cold shoulder.

Alina thinks I'm a zombie at the café, just doing the necessary back and forth but with no pep. I try to tell her I didn't have pep before, but she swears there's something missing.

I need to do something, need to act. Maybe going out is the right choice. Get some drinks in me, loosen me up a bit.

A few weeks ago, I had a similar urge and dyed my hair purple. Well, the highlights, at least. Jameson had mentioned it once. I had gone with the intentions of something drastic; a big chop or dying everything. But when my hairdresser asked me what I wanted to do, I hesitated before asking her to change the pink to a vibrant purple.

I don't love it, and it's not quite as bright as I was hoping. But it's almost like Jameson helped me because he wanted it. Which makes the ache in my chest worse every time I see them because I know he never will.

"Let's go out tonight." Alina bumps my shoulder. "Call Kylee and we'll go hit the club. It's discount drinks after nine."

"I don't know."

"Come on, Liv. You can't keep holing yourself up in your house. It's not going to bring him back. So, either go get him, or get the fuck out of the house."

She's right. Because I am holing away. After Jameson left and I calmed down, I found one button-down shirt I missed in my tantrum. Most nights, I find myself curled up on the couch with it, though at this point, the sandalwood scent is long gone from its fibers.

I don't know what else to do but wallow in misery.

"Okay. I'll go with you."

She jumps up and down, clapping. "Okay, awesome. Call Kylee too. We'll make it a night."

"Fine." I heave a sigh and shoot a quick text off to Kylee, but I know she'll be in. She's been begging me to go out with her in some way shape or form since Jameson left. An immediate answer of "Yesssss" is exactly what I was expecting.

Six hours later, I'm as dolled up as I'm willing to get in a pair of black jeans and a tight red t-shirt. Sneakers finish off the outfit that would normally have heels, but I just don't have it in me to put them on.

The club holds little fun. Alina and Kylee flank me, but I can't get myself to leave the bar. Any guy who comes over, they quickly thwart attempts, but it's not long before I feel like I'm holding them back.

"You guys go have fun. I'm fine here." I curl my tongue around my straw and take a sip of my Malibu Bay Breeze. A small smile is all it takes for them to look at each other, nod, and take off into the crowd.

I know they've been wanting to dance since we arrived, but they were being good friends and staying close. I can't feel guilty on top of the memories filtering through my mind. This is where Jameson and I first got together.

That spot is where he came up to me and then we kissed.

They couldn't have known. Or at least couldn't know the extent of how much it still pains me. Mostly because I don't let them in on the inner workings of my mind, or my heart. Yes, they know I'm still in love and still hurting, but they don't know the extent of it.

Part of why I wanted to come was a bit masochistic. I wanted the pain of the memories, I wanted to see if they'd flood my mind and rekindle those emotions from that day.

But now they have and it's more than I can take.

"I need to get out of here."

Slipping from my barstool, I leave the club without telling Alina or Kylee I'm going. I just need to leave, get some fresh air.

As I step out into the cool night air, it's damp, having rained and continuing to mist.

The weather is befitting of my mood.

The café. That's where I need to go. If I'm going to drown in memories, I may as well go to the place that has the second most, my house having the most of all.

I let myself in and trail my fingers along the counter, the tables. I sit at the one that became ours.

Then I make my way over to the counter, hopping up and staring down at the espresso machine like it's my mortal enemy. That's when the tears invade.

When I've finally had enough sobbing, I leave, walking back into the cooler and damp night, ready to head home.

But a loud horn blares and pain like I've never felt slams into my body.

Chapter 32
Jameson

The buzzing on my desk draws my attention. Where the fuck is my phone? Rifling through the papers, I find the glow buried under half of the Anderson contract.

Why the hell is Mazie calling me? Liv programmed her siblings into my phone, and I haven't had the heart to delete any of them.

"Hello?"

"Jameson."

"What's going on, Mazie? Why are you calling?"

I haven't heard from Liv in ten weeks. Not since she told me to leave and never come back. And there hasn't been a single day I haven't woken up thinking about her, that I haven't gone to bed wishing I was wrapped around her delicate frame. Every time I get coffee, anywhere, it never measures up.

"Jameson. It's Liv."

I'm on my feet at the mention of her name. "What happened?"

"She was in an accident, Jay. It's...it's bad. She's in the hospital."

The papers in my hand go fluttering to the ground, and with them, so does my heart.

"What hospital?"

"Memorial."

"I'll be there in..." I flick out my watch. It's after eleven at night. What the hell was she doing out this late? The café closes at eight. "I'll be there in two hours. Tops." I can take the jet, or the Corvette. I'll wrack up a dozen tickets to get there if I have to. But I'm going.

"Jay, don't come. I didn't call you so you'd come. I called you because, despite every fiber of my being saying otherwise, I felt like you should know."

"Two hours, Maze." I hang up before she can argue with me again. Her hatred of me isn't a secret, but I don't care right now. All I can think about is getting to Liv.

And I'm going to get there as fast as I can.

Quickly forming a messy pile on my desk, I make sure to grab everything I need to leave. My phone, my keys, my wallet. I toss some clothes into a duffel bag, which I throw over my shoulder, and then I'm running down to the car.

Thankfully, it's late and traffic is light, but I make my way toward Liv at record speeds.

It's all I can think about, getting to her, seeing her, holding her. I don't even know if she's moved on; maybe there's a new man there holding her hand, but I have to get to her.

I'll deal with that later.

Seeing Liv is all that's important. Making sure she's okay. There are things I can do for her, financially, that her family can't, and I'm going to ensure that she has the best care I can get her. Even if that means transferring her to another hospital.

"Slow down, Jameson. Get to her first. Maybe it's not as bad as Mazie made it seem." No. It's probably worse. Mazie doesn't exaggerate. And she wouldn't have called me if she didn't think it was a bad situation.

Something inside Mazie is scared about losing her sister and she wanted me to know before it was too late so that I could...I don't know. See her? Pay my respects? She told me not to come, but surely, she knew the second I heard Liv was in the hospital I'd be there in a heartbeat. I'd have teleported if I could.

Instead, I race through the night up the highway and to my girl. Because she'll always be *my* girl.

Chapter 33
Liv

*O*uch.

That's all I can think. Everything hurts, and my limbs are leaden.

Cracking open my eyes is a horrible idea, and stabbing white heat slams into my head when the light hits my retinas.

Trying to move just causes blinding fire to shoot through my body.

Pressure in my hand causes me to rip it away, pulling a scream from my lungs and tearing at my arid throat, sending the burning pain roaring through me.

Squeezing my eyes shut seems to cause more pain and a whimper that's foreign and distant sounds, but I quickly realize it came from me.

I don't remember what happened or where I am, but the pain everywhere tells me it's something bad. The sniffling I can distinguish over the beeping of machines reinforces this thought.

I can't open my eyes or mouth to look or speak.

So, I let myself sink back into the dark oblivion that starts as warmth coursing through my veins. Slowly, the feeling of comfort overtakes me, and I let it wash me away.

At least now the pain in my body matches the one in my heart.

Chapter 34
Jameson

The first thing I do is get Liv her own room. All her family is here, and that extends beyond her siblings to close friends. Money has rarely been a problem for me, as I've certainly thrown it around like candy. But I'd spend every last cent on Liv. I never thought it would be a consideration, but I'd live a poor existence if I could live it with her.

"We did an MRI of her brain to see if she had any signs of significant damage, any signs of a serious problem. Thankfully, we didn't see more than a rather large concussion, but we won't really know more until she wakes up."

My arms are crossed against my chest, one hand picking at my lip as I hunch over to hear the doctor. "And when might that be?"

"Hard to say."

Nodding like a moron who doesn't understand English seems to be all I can do at the moment.

"Well, I guess we'll wait then. I'd like regular updates."

"Mr. Penshir, I'm sorry, but you're not family. I already said too much, but that was at the allowance of the family." I stiffen at his utterance of the word they all hate. It's almost a reflex at this point.

"I just made a substantial donation to your hospital here, so you can give me updates. Or I'd be happy to take it up with the head of the hospital."

"I'll be sure to check in the with family frequently." Bowing, he starts to back away.

"Doctor. Don't use that word with them please."

He turns back to me, brow furrowed. "Which word would that be, Mr. Penshir?"

"Family." A chill rattles down my spine as I say it. "Use any other words. Siblings and friends, next of kin, anything else. Just, not that word."

"I can do that, Mr. Penshir. I'll check in within the next few hours."

Turning back to Liv's new room, Mazie is sitting next to her bed, holding her hand as her shoulders shake. Zachary, a local cop who's her best friend, is standing right behind her, his fingers tracing lightly up and down her spine.

Alina is standing across from the bed, curled into the side of Eli, who's shushing her. This family has been through more than anyone should have to go through in their lifetime. And yet, here's another bump in the road.

Stepping into the room, I feel the air still. None of them are fans of mine. I'm not exactly sure why, never have been. The breakup didn't help matters, of course.

While I know I'm not welcome, there's no way in hell I'm leaving. I know she'll be okay with her siblings, that she's in the best place for her, and now she has her own room. But there's no way I can leave her.

Taking a deep breath, I finally do what I have yet to be able to and look at Liv. *My* Liv. With just a glance, all the air is stolen from my lungs, blood freezes in my veins, and it takes any ounce of strength I have left not to collapse to the floor.

My strong, dominating girl, looks so tiny and frail, with tubes running in all directions. There's a cast and sling on her left arm, though that's not a surprise due to the breaks the doctor told me about. Even from the foot of her bed and the low lighting, I can make out a myriad of bruises on her face, chest, and arms.

All of that is more than enough to stop my heart, but what really seals the deal is when I take in her hair. I have to do a double take to make sure I'm seeing it clearly. Where pink streaks had so clearly been weeks ago, now are purple.

With a groan, I double over, my hands on my knees as my eyes mist. Breathing is nearly impossible as I gulp for air. A hand on my back makes me jump and I realize that Mazie has stood and is now comforting me. Me, of all people. I'm pretty sure she's my number one hater in life, and I have a lot.

"Sit, Jameson." It's a command, not a request.

Raising my head to look at her, I find nothing but kindness in her eyes, which shocks me like nothing else.

When she raises an eyebrow, I quickly oblige, taking the chair she had been occupying and taking Liv's hand between both of mine. Kissing along her knuckles, the wetness in my eyes overflows and drips onto her pale skin. I rest her fingers against my forehead and try to take a few deep breaths to calm the emotions trying to overwhelm me.

I've never been an emotional person. But I love this woman with every fiber of my being, and I don't know what I would do if I lost her. We may have broken up, but at least I knew she still existed out there in the world somewhere. That maybe, someday, we would be able to make our way back to each other. If tonight had gone even just a little bit differently, none of that would have been possible. I can't even begin to imagine how dark the world would be without Liv in it.

Having calmed myself enough to breathe at a regular rate, I lift my head and look back at Liv. I don't even care about her family behind me and reach out to brush some hair from her forehead, my fingers twisting into a lock of purple and sliding down to the ends.

About a week before she kicked me out, we'd been lying in bed, a lazy and naked morning. I was twisting a pink curl through my fingers while she rested sprawled on my chest, the sheet just barely covering her perfect ass.

"Have you ever considered a color other than pink?"

"I'm pretty sure I've considered all the colors. But my hair is so dark, I really wanted something that would pop. Something that would make me stand out." Of course she did. How could she ever blend into the background?

I had taken her chin in my hand and tilted her toward me. "Trust me, baby, you stand out all on your own, even without the bright hair." I leaned down and pressed my lips to hers.

"What color would you like for me?"

"Hm, I don't know. Maybe blue?" Squinting, I had looked at her hair. "No, not blue. Definitely not green. Purple. I think purple would look good. But not bright. More subtle. It would match your eyes."

"Mm, maybe a little bright. And you know they're not actually purple right?"

"They look like it in the right light. And I love it, because they're gorgeous, just like you. Would you change your hair for me? Because I do like the pink. It suits you, baby."

She had lifted a shoulder as she resumed her position with her head on my chest, swirling her finger up and down my side. "I don't know. Maybe. Change is good sometimes."

A throat clearing behind me pulls me from my reverie. The lock of purple is still between my fingers. Mazie may not have known it when she stood, but I'm not leaving this chair.

"I'm here, baby, I'm here. And I'm not going anywhere." I pull her fingers to my lips again.

Hours stack on top of hours as I sit and wait for Liv to wake up. The doctor made it clear that it might be a while.

Her family takes turns sitting, leaving, getting food. But I refuse to stand from this spot on the chair, refuse to take my hand or eyes off of her. I barely even acknowledge somebody else when they speak to me or enter the room.

I think the word deranged was thrown out once when they thought I couldn't hear but I don't care. All that matters is the woman lying prone in front of me.

The heaviness of my eyelids barely registers, the ache in my bones a distant memory. My body is running off of the need for Liv to be okay, for her to wake up and show me those beautiful, shining purple irises. To see her breathtaking smile.

More chairs are brought in so everybody can sit. Zach leaves at some point to go to work. I keep my eyes on Liv the whole time.

The sun rises and falls, and I can only tell by the way the shadows cast over Liv's face. But Liv doesn't move, not more than the steady rise and fall of her chest, thankfully unaided by machines.

It's not until darkness has overtaken that a flutter of her eyelids catches my attention.

I practically jump up from my chair and slam the call button.

All the breath leaves my lungs as her eyes lock on mine.

Chapter 35
Liv

The pain is at a dull level as the doctor looks me over. A bright light shines in my eyes, things are pushed on and prodded, which cause me to wince.

But aside from following the flashlight, I keep my gaze on Jameson.

Jameson.

What the hell is he doing here?

It's clear I'm in the hospital. That something happened, but the details are fuzzy.

Somebody had to have called him. But why? Nobody likes him, nobody has been on his side.

It must have been Alina. She was the closest thing to a friend he had in the family. But why? Was it that shaky? Was I close to dying?

"What's your name?"

"Olivia Baker. Liv."

Jameson's got his arms crossed over his chest while he stands on the far side of the room, leaning against the wall with my siblings huddled in the corner.

"What year is it?"

"Twenty, twenty-two."

"What town do you live in?"

"Juniper Grove."

These questions are getting old. I know they're just checking my mental capacity, but if they let me talk, they'd know more.

"Do you remember what happened that brought you here?"

"No. Not really. I was out with my friends. That's all I know."

The doctor nods resolutely and puts his stethoscope back into his pocket. "It may not feel like it with the amount of pain you're in, but you're quite lucky, Miss Baker. You were hit by a car, which has resulted in a few broken ribs, a broken wrist and clavicle, as well as a concussion. But it could have been far worse."

The litany of problems makes my breath catch, and I see pain flicker across Jameson's face as he leans forward, like it pains him to hear.

"Can I be alone with my visitors, please?"

"Of course. If you need anything, please don't hesitate to buzz us."

I nod, but still don't tear my gaze from Jameson. The monitor starts to beep louder as my heart picks up in speed. The doctor hesitates, but I assure him I'm okay.

It's more because of the conversation that's about to happen rather than how I'm feeling. Because while everything hurts, it's dull. I can feel the warmth of whatever pain meds they've given me still twisting through my body, making my head a touch fuzzy and my eyelids heavy.

With a deep breath, I prepare myself.

Chapter 36
Jameson

The doctor left five minutes ago, and nobody has said a word or even moved a muscle.

"What is he doing here, Maze? Who called him and why?"

"You were in an accident, Liv. Despite what I think about him, he loves you, and you love him. He deserved to know." Mazie takes a step forward and owns up to her actions.

"He's just going to leave again! Don't you get it? He doesn't want to be here; his job is more important than I am, and it always will be." She's borderline hysterical, and I contemplate getting a nurse to sedate her before she hurts herself.

"You don't know that, Liv. He had a right—"

"Actually," I interrupt. What I have to say may calm her. I hope it will, or there really is no hope left for me. "I'm quitting, Liv."

Her mouth falls open, and she's silent.

"The second Mazie told me you were in the hospital, that you'd been in an accident and it was bad, that was the moment I decided. No job is more important than you. *Nothing* is more important than you."

"But...but you hate this town."

"I do." I take a step closer to her.

"I won't leave."

"I know." Another step closer.

"You'll resent me for having to live here." Her voice is becoming wavery again.

"I won't." Another step. Now I'm close enough that I can grasp her toes, which I do.

All she can do is nod, just before her eyes overflow and her head falls into her hand. I'm by her side, resting on her bed in half a second, pulling her head to my chest and kissing her temple.

"I'm here, baby. I'm not leaving you, not ever, not for anything or anyone. You, Liv, are all that matters to me in this life." The urge to squeeze her is strong, but I fight it, not wanting to hurt her. Instead, I wrap my arms around her, cupping her head and cradling it against my shoulder. "I love you, Liv. I love you so much."

Her fingers tighten in my shirt as she shakes in my hold, her chest rattling.

"I've got you, Liv. It's okay."

"He hasn't left in days, Liv. And you know I'm the first to say he's a piece of shit, but he hasn't left your side. Suit and all," Mazie adds.

She pulls away and looks down at my crumpled suit. "Who?"

"Brioni."

Her eyes widen. Our running joke of my suit names and who was most expensive clearly returns. Grabbing my sleeve, her eyes fill again, her full bottom lip trembling. Sliding my thumb across it, I lean in to close my mouth over hers.

Tears wet my cheeks as they spring from her eyes. For some strange reason, I know this is one of the things that shows her how much she means to me. That I sat here for days in the same expensive suit not worrying about the wrinkles or the appearance.

I'm going to let her pick two or three of her favorites and donate the rest. I won't need them anymore. But I do want to be able to take her to fancy dinners, to whisk her away somewhere at a moment's notice. There's always a reason to own at least one suit.

Shifting to my other side, I lay her back gently, resting alongside her. She curls into my chest, her free hand twisting into my lapels where she can reach them as she shudders with sobs.

"Shh, it's okay, baby. I'm right here."

"You left." Accusation twines its way through the sobs.

"You threw me out. Literally. You threw all my shit in the yard." A light laugh works through with my words, because if I really think about it, it is kind of funny. But only now that I have her back in my arms.

"I'm sorry."

"I should have called your bluff. I should have insisted on staying. I'm sorry I left and was gone for so long. But I'm here now, and I'm never leaving you again. You hear me? Never."

She presses her head against my sternum and adjusts herself until I have to lie flat and she's practically on top of me. Her ear is pressed over my heart, her tears wetting my shirt under her cheek.

Within minutes of lying in this position, with my hand smoothing down her hair, pulling a curl straight, and back up again, the sobs have ceased, and her breaths have leveled out.

Glancing up, I find everybody looking at us with shock and awe on their faces. Alina's eyes are shimmering, Mazie's lip is trembling, and Elijah looks like he wants to buy me a beer. When Mazie clasps her hands in front of her and nods, the tears fall, and she has to cup her mouth to keep from making a sound.

I know Liv is asleep on me by her steady, deep breaths and tiny twitches. I'll stay like this for days if it keeps her comfortable, if it helps her sleep and rest.

"How are we doing in here?" Doctor Ruggins returns to the room.

"She seems to be asleep again. Is that okay? Or should she be awake?"

"It's fine for her to sleep, good even. Her body needs rest, even with a concussion. We want to watch for any major mood changes, any forgetfulness, persistent headaches. Darker rooms and low noise situations are going to be best for her for a few days. You'll want to wake her up every two hours to make sure she's rousable and coherent."

"And her lying like this? Is it alright?" I gesture gently down at Liv, not wanting to jostle too much.

"If she's comfortable, it's fine. For the wrist, collarbone, and ribs it's about comfort. She'll need help dressing, bathing, and possibly other tasks. But unless she's having pain, she's fine to sleep how she prefers, including like this."

Looking around the room, he takes in the five disheveled people. "You all should get some sleep too. Mr. Penshir, she'll be fine if you want to head elsewhere for the night."

Tightening my arms around her, I settle in and close my eyes. "I'm perfect right where I am."

Murmurs make me lift my very heavy eyelids to look at the siblings. They're gathered at the back of the room, talking amongst themselves, Zachary standing just beside Mazie, his hand on her lower back. Of course the whole force had heard about Liv's accident, and they urged him to take the time off and return.

Liv swears there's nothing there, but I have to disagree. At least from Zach's side, there are definite feelings.

"You guys can all go home. I'm not leaving her, and I'll call if anything changes. I've got her, guys. Please go get some rest."

"Jameson, you need rest too. You came in in the middle of the night a few nights ago and haven't left." The softness in Mazie's tone shocks me to no end.

"Neither have any of you."

"She's our sister," Eli chimes in like that means more than what Liv is to me. They may be blood, but that requires them to stay. I'm staying because I love her more than life itself.

"And she's the love of my life. I'm not leaving, so arguing with me is pointless. If you want to stay, stay. But it's not necessary. I'm sure you'd all like a hot shower and comfortable bed to sleep in." While all of those things sound amazing to me, there's nowhere else I'd rather be.

"Okay. You're right, Jameson. But make sure you call if anything happens." Mazie gathers her things as she starts to leave and jerks her head toward the door for all to follow. Though she's second born, she's the leader of the pack.

On their way out, all stop by the bed to give Liv a kiss. It's a little awkward, having them so close to me. But they all give me an acknowledgement as well. Eli pats my shoulder, Mazie gives a smile and touches my hand, Alina puts her hand on my forearm and squeezes, tossing in a wink. Even Zach gives a gentle punch to my upper arm.

When they all leave, I adjust, shimmying down the bed a bit and lowering the back. Liv whines for a moment, but I quickly shush her and go back to stroking her hair.

Despite the caustic smell in the room, the scent of Liv filters into my nose and I'm immediately at peace. Her warmth, the feel of her heart beating against my chest, her persistent breaths, all remind me she's here, she's alive, and we're together.

Everything will be okay if we're together.

Chapter 37
Liv

"**W**here were you, Liv? Why were you out so late?" It's been two days since I woke up and Jameson hasn't left my side.

He hasn't gone to change, shower, eat, nothing. If food isn't brought to him, I share or he goes without. He sponge bathes in the bathroom. It's kind of incredible and exactly what I need. It shows me he's here to stay.

But for the past two days, he's been wanting to know what happened. It's still hazy, but I can give him the lead up.

My chin drops to my chest. "I had gone out, to the club where we exchanged names. I was in a bad place, trying to relive memories. After the club didn't work, I left. There are so many memories, Jameson. It hurt to be at work, day after day. It was like a knife to my chest. Every corner holds something. I swear, when it was really quiet, I could almost hear you calling me 'Sweetheart' again."

Staring at the ceiling, I try to will the tears away but it's no use.

"I don't even know how long I was in there reliving things, replaying them in my head while I sat on the counter and sobbed. For weeks after you left, I could barely use the espresso machine. I made Alina stop making the lemon drop muffins, because I just, I couldn't see them or smell them or hear them be ordered in a voice that wasn't yours." I turn away at the memories. So many accommodations my sister made for me.

"Eventually, I left the café, but it was late, and pitch black outside. I was so distracted, I didn't see the car coming."

"You live in a tiny ass town, and everybody knows every damn detail about everybody else. Who the fuck would have hit you?"

I put my hand on his forearm to try to calm him. I can practically feel his blood boiling and see the steam billowing from his ears.

"It was some tourist. It wasn't that horrendous, Jameson. He didn't run me down or anything. It was an accident. And honestly, probably as much my fault as his, because I didn't even look for a car in the road before stepping out."

He rests his forehead against mine. "Somebody hurt you, Liv. I'm ready for a head on a platter."

"I know. But I'm okay. Especially because you're here." Unease settles into my body. He's said he's not leaving, but was that temporary? We're waiting for my discharge papers so I can go home. But is he also leaving? Was this just because I'm hurt?

"I'm not leaving, baby. Not unless you tell me to...again. But next time, I'm fighting harder to stay. I'm not taking your response so easily. And I'm certainly not listening to any of your siblings." Relief floods me with his words, like he's read my mind.

"I'll never tell you to leave again. I'm not strong enough to do that again. And nobody will say anything. They're all team Jameson now. They were even before you came back."

Through much discussion and some arguments, they were able to see the error of their ways. Even Mazie, who had to come the furthest and maybe hadn't really crossed all the way. Alina had always liked Jameson, and Eli quickly grew to like him after they first met. Mazie was the hold up, and after one late night chat and after her conversation with Eli that night he left, she mostly turned her leaf.

"Good, I'm glad. They're going to have to get used to me in their life, because I'm in yours for as long as you'll have me."

"You're really shutting down your business?" There's an ounce of hesitance with my question. Part of me doesn't want to hear the answer because I feel guilty that he's doing it for me. He worked hard to build what he has.

"I am. I don't really need it, Liv, not like I need you. I have plenty of money and I'm going to be with somebody who has one third of her own very successful business. And while I won't be working, I won't lose my skills so I can always help make sure that business *stays* successful." He's going to go crazy with nothing to do. Maybe I can convince him to consult. To help other businesses in Juniper Grove and even Pineville City. It won't be the same as the big city, but it's better than nothing.

"What are you going to do when I get out of here?"

"Take you home."

"And then?"

"Draw you a bath, climb in with you, wash you, and take you to bed for hours of kissing." Mmm. Every second of that sounds incredible.

"I mean your things, Jameson. What about your things?"

"I don't need any of them." He must be joking. His entire apartment is full of belongings. What does he plan to do with them?

"Clothes? You don't need clothes?"

"I have a small duffel in the car. I'll buy new things."

"What about your apartment?" My pulse is climbing as I think about all the things he has, that he'll have to leave to get them, that maybe he'll change his mind.

He cups my cheek and rubs his thumb along my skin. "Hey, take a breath. We'll figure it all out, together. I was actually thinking of keeping the apartment. Letting it be a playground of sorts for us." That sounds like an amazing idea.

"Really? Can you afford that?"

"Sweetheart, I can afford to buy the building and then burn it to the ground and not think twice about it." The fact that he has that much money is shocking but doesn't change anything.

"The suits? You're my suit...you need to keep them." My fingers twist in the lapel of his crumpled jacket. This one may be beyond repair.

"After you're settled, and healed, and we're back on track, we're taking a trip there again. You get to pick three or so that you like the best. The rest can go." I love that he's letting me make the decision for which suits he keeps. I'll have to pick the best ones, of course.

"Miss Baker? Are you ready to go?" A nurse comes in at that moment, holding a stack of papers in her hands.

"Yes, finally."

Signing the forms as quickly as I can, Jameson and I leave the hospital, hand in hand.

"You know this car doesn't really fit in here." One corner of my lip tips down as I consider the bright blue sports car. It sticks out amongst the Hondas and Toyotas. There are very few luxury brand vehicles in Juniper Grove.

"I'm not getting rid of the 'Vette, baby." He pulls me against him and kisses the top of my head.

"Okay, good, because I do love this car. But, maybe something a little more day to day?"

"Sure thing, Sweetheart." He gives me a wink as he opens my door and helps me in. Instead of shutting the door, he leans in and starts fussing with my seatbelt.

"Jay." I rest my palm against his cheek and watch the breath and tension release from him. Instead of answering, his head gently drops to my shoulder. This whole ordeal has taken a toll on him. "I'm okay. It's just a few breaks."

"It's four breaks, several bruises, a concussion, and...and..." His hand tightens on my thigh, and he presses his head against my shoulder. "I almost lost you, Liv."

"You didn't *almost* lose me, Jameson." He's being a bit overly dramatic. Yes, it was a bad accident that could have been worse, but he didn't almost lose me.

"I could have."

"We weren't even together."

"It doesn't matter. That doesn't matter. You not existing on this planet anymore, that matters. I'd feel that, I'd know. Not being with you these past ten weeks has been excruciating, but I knew you were still here, living your life, trying to make the most of it, and hopefully, at some point, being happy. Even if that wasn't with me, even if somebody brought you the happiness I wanted to give you, I was okay with that because, in my mind, I could picture your smile and laugh and know you were doing well."

Shifting in my seat, I loop my arm around his shoulders as he squats and buries his head in my lap, wrapping his arms around my waist and holding tight.

"You're not going to let me out of your sight for a while, are you." It's a statement more than a question because I know he's going to be my constant companion for the next short while.

He shakes his head, and I can't help but laugh. How we started out at such odds, and ended up here, I'm not sure I'll ever truly understand.

Canting my head to the side, I look down at him. This large man, crouched on the ground, curled into my lap and holding on for dear life. His hair has grown out since we last saw each other. Not a lot, as I'm sure he got it cut on his very strict two-week schedule, but enough that I can tell he's been struggling. I run my fingers through it when a thought comes to mind and rushes through my body, causing my heart to beat erratically.

"You know, my dad would have really liked you. Everybody thinks I don't know enough of what my parents would have liked for me or about me or who I've become. But I had more time with them than they realize. I'm a keen observer and take it all in. Mom always used to say I was a sponge, just sitting there absorbing everything around me. That includes how my parents were. *Who* they were. As well as what they saw in people."

Clearing my throat, I chase away the lump to forming. "After you left, I was in a really dark place. I didn't want to get out of bed, didn't want to go to work. I was rude to customers."

"You? Never."

I gently slap his back at his attempt at a joke. "I'm serious, Jameson. I was mean. Mazie and I got into a fight on the café floor and then didn't talk for two weeks. One night Eli came over to have what he called a heart-to-heart, but it was really his way of chastising me. After a long conversation over a few drinks, he said that he'd let Mazie sway his judgment of you at first too. Though, in time, he saw the benefits of you being part of my life.

"The night you left, Mazie and Eli had a conversation on my porch, and I listened to them talk about how Mom and Dad would have felt about you, and even Mazie admitted and could see that they would have liked you. It started to settle into my mind."

I keep running my fingers through his hair, and for a minute, I think he's fallen asleep, in this incredibly uncomfortable position, until he squeezes me.

"That night he came to give me a hard time, Eli reaffirmed it. He told me to come find you, Jameson, to go to your apartment, to talk to you. But I'm stubborn, which you well know. I didn't want to come back to beg you to be with me."

His head lifts, brows scrunched, and he takes my chin in his hand so our eyes meet. "You would *never* be begging me to be with you, Liv. I stayed away because of what Alina said, what Mazie said, what you said. All three of you pushed me away, made me feel I wasn't good enough for you. And you're all right, because I'm not."

I open my mouth to talk, but he holds up a hand to stop me.

"I'm a man who's been married to his job since day one. But the mere thought of never being able to see you again, never being able to accidentally, yet surely on purpose, run into you again was enough for me to quit. You're all I want in this life, Olivia Baker."

"Things won't be as hard for you going forward. Alina's always mostly liked you. Or at least, she wanted to. One thing this whole ordeal showed both of us is that we've let Mazie guide our decisions for far too long. No more. She worries about me, they all do. But she's promised to try to come around and not give you such a hard time."

Part of me feels like I need to convince him that my siblings are going to be easy on him for him to stay. Maybe I do to put my own mind at ease.

"It doesn't matter, Liv. I mean, it's nice she's going to try to be on board with us and not be on my ass all the time, but even if it was incredibly horrible and uncomfortable every day, it wouldn't matter."

"Oh, I'm sure she'll still be on your ass. It's who she is. But she's not going to chase you away."

"That's what I'm trying to say though, Liv. It wouldn't even be possible. There's nothing anybody can say or do to get me to leave you again. Ever."

Dipping his head, he nuzzles his nose into my hipbone, tightening his arms as much as he can while still leaving some space. "I'm not going to break if you hug me tightly, Jameson."

"You might."

"I won't. Just be gentle on my ribs, my arm. But my hips are fine."

"The giant bruise right here says otherwise." As he speaks, his left palm slides to the top of my hipbone and his lips press against the right.

Sighing, my chin drops to my chest. "Jameson, I'm okay. I'll heal and be fine."

"But you're not right now, Liv. You have no idea how many different times and ways this scenario has played over in my head since I got that phone call. How I could be here saying goodbye to you as we put you in the ground instead of feeling your warmth right now." His voice cracks as he talks and his heart hammers against my thigh.

I'll never be able to fully understand what it is he went through, how he's felt during all of this. Yes, we were broken up. But hadn't I always had the same thoughts and hopes for him? I knew he was out there, living his life, doing what he loves. The fact that it didn't involve me was like knives ever present in my body. But knowing he was out there, it was enough.

"Jameson."

"Yeah, baby?"

"I'm tired. Can we go home?"

When he doesn't move from my lap or answer me, I know he's hesitating.

"I promise I won't so much as blink without you being next to me. We can order food, though I'm sure Alina's already packed the fridge." If I know my sister, she's been cooking nonstop since the day she left the hospital, choosing to cook instead of showering and sleeping. It's what she does when she's stressed and worried, or really, feeling any emotion.

"I have to touch you, Liv."

"Uh, I know I said I'm okay, but I'm not exactly sure I'm feeling up for *that*. I mean, I did just—"

"No, Liv. I don't mean sexually. I just mean that I have to physically feel that you're here." Wow. He's so shaken up.

"Okay. I understand. We're going to have to have a discussion about this and your feelings and everything, but I understand it's a bit raw for now."

"I promise I won't be like this for long. I'll go back to being the asshole you love to hate. In all the ways I dreamt of getting you back, this wasn't even on the list. Getting a call from Mazie, of all people, telling me you were hurt...it was like an alternate universe."

As much as I want Jameson to get his feelings out, the medicine is starting to wear off. "We'll get through it. But, please, take me home. My shoulder is starting to hur—" I don't even finish the word before Jameson is standing, taking my legs and spinning me into the car. He literally runs to the driver's side and hops in.

Once the car is started and he has one hand tightly on my thigh, Jameson drives at a snail's pace back to my house.

"You know you didn't have to drive so slowly." Taking his hand, I let him pull me out of the car once we're parked in the driveway. "Mrs. Henderson passed us."

"She was speed walking."

"She's ninety years old, Jameson!"

"She's spritely." The pace doesn't stop as he walks me into the house, his arm around my waist and hand steadying my non-casted forearm.

"Jameson. Please. You're going to drive me crazy. I can walk, and you can drive faster than fifteen miles an hour."

"The speed limit is only twenty-five."

"So fifteen puts you ten miles under."

"Olivia, please. Just give me a few days. Give me some time. Please." He's begging me, and I hear the exhaustion in his voice. I take a moment to truly examine him and find him haggard, a beard growing haphazardly since he hasn't trimmed up in a while, and there are dark circles under his eyes.

"Okay, Jay. I'll give you a few days."

A heavenly scent wafts out the door the second it's open. My mouth instantly waters.

"Alina's been here," we say in unison, turning toward each other and laughing. But the laughing hurts, and I wince, putting my free hand at my side.

The horror in Jameson's eyes is enough to crack my heart. Putting my hand on his cheek, I run my thumb along his stubbled skin. "I'm okay, I'm okay. Just, maybe no laughing for a few days."

Walking into the kitchen, I don't even have to open the oven to know it's Alina's famous lasagna. It's an ultimate favorite of mine. She makes her own sauce and it's about as close to heaven as you can get while eating. Even still, I gingerly pick up the folded note that sits on the stove.

Jameson wraps his arm around my middle and presses his front to my back, resting his chin on my shoulder while he reads over it.

Sibby,

I know you don't want to read anything all gushy and mushy about how much we all love you, how scared we were that we were going to lose you, or how broken we'd all be had that happened. All I'm going to say is that we're Bakers, so you know we're here for you. With Jameson around, I'm sure you won't need anything, but if you do, please speak up. To any of us. You know I've already filled your fridge with your favorites. There are three doze n muffins in the pantry, along with your favorite chocolates, a fridge filled with the staples, and we got all your favorite drinks. Mazie also brought over your favorite coffees from the café to make sure you don't run out for as long as you'll be homebound for. We all agree, take your time. Don't rush back. If that's a few weeks, take it. Just let us know when you decide. We'll hold down the fort. Let me know when you decide you want to make the meatballs, and I'll bring over freshly baked bread. Eli tossed some clothes in your room for Jameson and said he'd pick up a few things this weekend in case Jameson can't get out.

We all love you, Liv, but we'll stay away until you call us in because we know you and Jameson need this time to reconnect.

-LeeLee

"You have a pretty amazing family, baby. Do you know that?" For the first time ever, I don't cringe at the use of "family." Because we are one, and now Jameson has been brought into the fold.

"I do."

Leaning my head back against his shoulder, he starts to sway us from side to side. Taking a look at the microwave, I see that there's a half hour left on the lasagna. Either Jameson and Alina have been in cahoots, or this town is using its chatterbox grapevine to keep tabs on me.

"Let's get changed. Maybe a quick shower?" He must have noticed the same thing I did.

"That sounds nice. But I have to cover my cast. Not sure I can figure that out in enough time to also shower."

The smile that spans his face is a mix of mischievous and proud, and it kind of freaks me out. "Don't worry about a thing, baby. I broke my arm when I was thirteen. And again when I was seventeen. I got this."

Looking through the cabinets, he pulls out a hidden plastic bag, then starts rifling through the junk drawer. Turning to look at me with a victorious look on his face, he holds out a plastic bag and rubber band.

"Can I do that? With my sling?"

"We'll have to take the sling off and you'll just keep your arm close to your body. I'll help you."

Trusting people is not something that comes to me readily. It didn't come with Jameson at first either. In fact, he had to fight hard to prove it to me, and when he left, it fractured the very foundation of the trust I'd built for him. But in the past few days, with him not leaving my bedside once, not even to eat, not only has that fracture been cemented over, but anything lost has been rebuilt and fortified.

Closing the gap between us, I rest my palm against his cheek and raise onto my toes to press my lips to his. "Thank you."

Leaning his head down, he rests his forehead against mine. Slipping my hand to hold the back of his neck, we stand in silence in the middle of the kitchen for a few minutes, breathing each other in.

"Come on, let's get clean, because we need to face the facts. We both stink. And then we should eat. Nothing really ever seems as dire after Alina's lasagna." Alina's lasagna is like a magical mixture of delicious pasta, meat, and cheese. It can cure almost anything that's ailing you. "Then I say we either go right to sleep or snuggle on the couch and watch a movie."

"How about we fall asleep cuddling on the couch while watching a movie?"

"Sounds like a plan to me."

The shower is invigorating and refreshing. I watch days' worth of grime wash down the drain with the bubbles. Jameson washes my hair, combing out the knots as gently as he possibly can, which after days in bed is a feat on its own. The care with which he washes me is nothing short of amazing. This man who was all edges when we met, rough in tone and how we interacted, is now soft and fluffy. At least where I'm concerned.

This is further enforced as he wraps a towel around me and holds my arm to guide me out of the shower stall.

Unable to tear my eyes from his glistening chest, a pulsation ricochets through my body and settling in my clit. I know it's going to be a *very* long few weeks. Especially knowing that Jameson is going to insist on at least washing me every time, if not also joining me.

While I'm practically drooling over his perfection, Jameson is all business. Well, now, at least. There may have been an extra few seconds of affection paid to my breasts, and as much as he tried to hide his erection, he couldn't. I didn't draw attention to it intentionally, understanding the situation at hand.

"Turn around, Liv, I'll do your hair."

"You can't do my hair, Jameson, you don't know how." It's a complex process of different hair products that I've perfected over the years.

"I think I've watched you do it enough times that I can figure it out."

Realizing I have no choice, I press my lips together and turn around, tipping my chin to the ceiling. The fruity scent of my leave-in conditioner wafts into my nose and Jameson starts working it through my tendrils. The gentle pull is oddly satisfying, and when he scrunches the curls to the base of my skull, I know he's trying his hardest. But it's not until he grabs the ratty t-shirt, one I stole from him, and eases my curls into it before scrunching again, that I know how closely he watched me the months we were together.

Snuggled into him on the couch, everything feels right with the world. I may have a broken wrist and clavicle, bruised ribs, and the trailing painful wisps of a horrendous headache, but *life* is good.

With my head on his chest, Jameson has his arm around me, his fingers twirling through my curls while a movie drones on in the background. We chose the first movie that had a decent preview, but neither of us is really invested.

"You really dyed your hair purple?" His voice is so low, I mostly hear the rumble through his pectoral than I do his mouth.

With his words, my heart gallops. I thought he hadn't noticed, or that he'd forgotten our conversation all those weeks ago. "Yeah, I did. I had to see what it looked like. I know I pushed you away, Jay, but I never stopped thinking about you. I never stopped hurting in your absence. The hair? It was one small thing I could do that felt like you were close."

"I like it."

Snuggling in deeper, I let my leaden eyelids close.

"Are you sure you're comfortable like that, baby? I don't want you to hurt. Or wake up hurting. Maybe we should go to bed." He's already shifting to get up from the couch.

"I'm okay just like this. I promise."

Sighing heavily, but clearly acquiescing, he resumes playing with my hair, extending the curls as he trails his fingers down my spine.

"Alright then. Sleep, Sweetheart. I'll be right here if you need anything."

"Okay. I love you." The words come out mumbled as I can barely get my mouth to form them.

"I love you too, Liv. More than you could ever truly know."

Chapter 38
Jameson

While my eyes feel like the desert and my head aches from exhaustion, I can't sleep. Liv's been zonked out on me for at least an hour now, probably more. But sleep eludes me.

There are too many things racing through my mind. It's like dogs chasing each other around a room. So many thoughts running circles, trying to be the top place. Only one thing will calm it all.

Reaching carefully for my phone on the table, I find it's only nine at night. Early, all things considered, but incredibly late taking into account the past few days. Swiping it open, I flip to the contact I need.

Hey man. I need a hookup. Price doesn't matter. Do me a solid and let me know what you can do for me. I need this done ASAP.

The return message comes faster than I expected.

You got it. I'll reach out when it's done.

No questions. Good.

A weight has been lifted from my shoulders, and my chest feels lighter. At least one thing will be in place.

There's another piece of business I'd love to take care of, but it requires a face to face, and I'm not sure how to do that without leaving Liv, which isn't a possibility.

I have every intention of marching myself straight into the police station and sitting down with Zach. What good is a cop who's close to the family if he can't handle things like this? Why is the fucker who hit my girl not in jail?

Actually, forget this. Flipping to Mazie's name, red starts to encroach my vision.

Me: I need Zach's number.

Mazie: Why?

Me: I just do. Please

Mazie: Jameson, everything was done by the book. It was an ACCIDENT and I can assure you that Zach loves Liv like a sister and would protect her if there was anything more to be done.

Me: Somebody hit her Mazie.

Why am I having to explain this to her? It's her sister, for Christ's sake.

The phone vibrates in my hand and the screen lights up with Mazie's face. Liv had programmed all of her siblings' faces to go with their numbers.

Rolling my eyes and sighing heavily, my lips press tightly together, and I consider ignoring it. Swiping the green phone, I pull the phone to my ear.

"There's nothing that can be done, Jameson." I like that I don't have to say anything for her to talk.

"He hit her, Mazie." Speaking quietly, but firmly, I enunciate every syllable.

"I know, Jameson. I know. And trust me, I went over it with Zach extensively. There's an accident report, he admitted fault, he got his ticket, and has paid her medical bills." All except the room, which I took care of. And if a single bill comes through, I'll take care of that too.

"We almost lost her, Mazie. Doesn't that mean anything to you? To Zach? He claims to love her like a brother and yet lets things be this way?" Screw what's expected and by the book. Go after him where it hurts. Because he hurt my girl.

"We didn't almost lose her, Jameson. She was hurt, and yes, it could have been far worse. But it wasn't. Listen, Liv wasn't entirely faultless in this either. The cop on the scene wanted to question it, but the guy felt horrible, and Zach showed up and intervened to make sure nothing was placed on Liv."

Rage boils under my skin. "What's his name?"

"Who?"

"The officer on the scene." How dare he want to place blame on my girl after she'd been hit by a car and was on her way to the hospital. What sort of moron? I'll have his damn badge.

"You know I'm not going to tell you that."

"We have to do *something*."

Liv stirs and pushes against my chest to sit up with her good hand.

"I have to go." Hitting the end button, I toss the phone to the side before Mazie even responds. "Hey, baby, you feeling okay?"

"I'm a little sore, actually. But what was that about?"

"What was what about?"

Canting her head to the side, Liv raises an eyebrow. "Really? You're going to pretend you didn't wake me up by giving somebody a hard time? It sounded like Mazie."

"I just wanted Zach's phone number."

Her whole body sags, and she rests her forehead against my chest while heaving a sigh. Shaking her head, she pushes up to sitting, putting her hand on my cheek. Meeting her eyes, their normal color is overshadowed by pain and the shimmer of fresh tears. "I'm so sorry I put you through all of this."

My heart drops when the tears spill over. Cupping the back of her neck, I pull her to me, resting my lips against her forehead. "You didn't do this, Liv. Somebody else did."

"I wasn't paying attention."

"Baby, he *hit* you." The words come through gritted teeth. I'm ready to go for blood.

"I know. But I wasn't paying attention. You need to hear me, Jameson. This wasn't some tragic, run me down in the middle of the road incident. It was late, I wasn't looking for cars or even aware of my surroundings, and somebody hit me. That person stopped, called 911, and stayed. He's also checked in to make sure I was okay. Which I am."

"But it could have gone so differently. This asshole needs to know that."

"I'm sure he does. And it didn't go differently. You can't keep living in this 'what if' world. Because that world doesn't exist. This one does." Resting her palm firmly over my heart, I close my hand around hers. "I'm here, I'm alive. A little banged up, sure. But I will be good as new before you know it."

I do know. The doctor confirmed, repeatedly, that Liv will be just fine. After she gets her cast and sling off, she may need some physical therapy to get full range of motion and use, but it's temporary. The concussion will have no long-lasting effects, and any other breaks and bruises will disappear, like nothing ever happened.

That's the part I have a hard time dealing with. How can we act like nothing ever happened? How can we move on and let this just be a part of her story? She's been through enough without this whole ordeal.

Turning my face back to hers, I realize she's right. She will be fine. *We* will be fine.

Brushing the hair from her cheeks and tucking it behind her ears, I look over her face. It may be bruised and discolored, and slightly swollen in places, but she's still stunning. "You know I love you, right?"

"Yes."

"And I'm serious about quitting."

"I don't want you to quit your job, Jameson. I just...I've lost too many people I love." Wait. She doesn't want me to quit? That's an entirely different conversation to have. I thought it's what she wanted from me.

"I know. And if you'll have me, I'd love to stay here, as long as you want me to."

"Well, then I guess I should clear out your drawers and part of the closet again. But what about everything you have in the city? And you need to work."

"When you're healed and feeling better, we'll take a trip and pack up anything I want or need to keep and bring it back. I was thinking of keeping the apartment so we could go for trips now and again. And I don't actually *need* to work." We had this conversation, but I'm taking the fact that she's been on massive pain meds as her reason for forgetting.

"Oh right, mister filthy rich. But you can't just sit around all day. It's not in your nature. And I do still have to work." She's right. I'll lose my mind with nothing to do all day.

"No, baby, you don't. Not financially, at least."

"Jameson. I need to. It's my business, my sister's business. In some ways, it's my parents' legacy."

"How about we figure out things when you're better. Taking care of you is my priority, everything else can wait."

"You really want to move? To this tiny little shit town?" Her eyebrows lift high on her forehead, as though she's truly challenging me.

"I do. Because the woman I love lives here, and as much as she acts like she hates it, I know she really loves it. Especially because the *people* she loves are here. I can't take that away from her."

"You'd really do all of that, just for me?"

"Of course I would. Liv, all I want is to wake up to you every morning, to go to sleep curled around you every night. I always have, I just couldn't see how to have both the career I've established and the woman with the life I want. And then your accident happened, and it immediately made me realize you are all that matters. I can do my job from anywhere, can limit the travel to what *I* want. I'm sorry I didn't see that sooner." We let things fall in the middle and get muddled when they should have been crystal clear.

At least they are now.

"Going through the kind of tragedy I have, you start to believe that everything happens for a reason, even if only because you have to."

A large yawn takes over, and then Liv flinches, clutching her wrist against her chest.

"You hurting, baby?" Reaching for my phone, I check the time. "It's a little early for your pain meds, think you can hold on for another hour?"

"Mhm. I'm okay, just the stretch made my collarbone hurt."

"Want to try to sleep some more?"

"Maybe just watch a show?"

"Sure, anything you want." Wrapping my arm around her waist, she snuggles into my shoulder as I find something to watch. Leaning back against the cushions, I kiss the top of her head and start twirling purple curls. It's not the most comfortable, but it beats the hospital chair.

The sound of Liv whining and crying causes me to stir, and I quickly realize, we both fell asleep. Forcing my lids open, I find her next to me, huddled in on herself and clutching her wrist.

Fuck. Day one at home and I've already screwed this up and let her down.

"Baby, you're okay. I'm right here." I reach out to touch her and then hesitate. Maybe it hurts too much for that. I wasn't with her at first, but Eli had said she didn't want to be touched the few times she was awake. "Hang on. Just, hang on, Liv."

Jumping up, I practically run to the kitchen, grabbing a fresh glass of water and her pain medicine. Sitting back on the couch as close to her as I can, I put the water on the table and shake out a pill. "Here, baby, take this. You'll feel better."

Tears streaming down her cheeks, making my heart wrench and giving me the strong urge to punch myself in the face, she takes the water and tentatively brings it to her lips. Swallowing down the pill with a shaky hand, she puts the cup on the table and leans into me.

"I'm sorry, Sweetheart, I'm so sorry. I fell asleep and missed the time. Next time, I'll do better. I promise." Grabbing my phone from the table, I set alarms for every six hours.

"Just hold me until it stops." Her words come out with nothing but whines and my chest aches. I let her down.

"Of course." Leaning back, I pull her down against my chest, shushing her while I play with her hair and trail my fingers down her spine. She told me once that it was soothing, and that's what she needs right now.

The wetness pooling on my shirt and the tiny whimpers that come every few seconds are like knives stabbing in my heart.

Thankfully, it's not too long before it's just hitching breath, that quickly starts to even out. The doctor had said the pills would work quickly and make her tired. Right now, I'm eternally grateful for that.

For a brief moment, I debate whether to stay here or move Liv to the bedroom. But the decision is easy.

Scooping her up in my arms, I carry Liv down the hall to her room. Our room. Usually, she prefers to sleep in just a big t-shirt and panties, though sometimes just the shirt. But I don't want to wake her, so I set her down on her side of the bed, running my hand over the top of her head.

The moment I'm settled on my side, Liv moves in my direction. Not wanting her to hurt herself, I wrap my arm around her and place her head on my chest. When she stills completely, I know she's back to sleep.

For ten weeks, this is everything I've missed. And while this is not at all the way I wanted it back, I'm eternally grateful to be back with my girl.

Chapter 39
Liv

It's been three weeks and wearing a cast is becoming more annoying by the day. Jameson's getting pretty good at doing my hair, but the rest of it is old. It itches, having to put a bag on every shower is tedious, and I'm pretty sure it's starting to smell.

Jameson is still my constant shadow, which I love to an extent, but he's gotten better about not watching my every single breath. He took the doctor's orders very seriously and woke me up every two hours that first night, but I begged him to let me sleep more, which he agreed to pretty quickly. The poor man was exhausted.

While my bruises have turned a yellowish green or have disappeared, and much of the swelling has gone down, there's still a lot of pain in my wrist and shoulder. It's not so extreme that I need to be on my pain pills every six hours, but if I go too long or move too much, it still hurts.

The hardest part is not being physical with Jameson. At this point, it's beyond a need. But he refuses to even touch me in a remotely sexual way. The most I get is a heated makeout session, which is great when my lips are sore and swollen, but not enough when my clit is too.

"Jay, I won't break if you touch me." This comes after another heavy makeout session where I'm left with wanting more than anything else.

"I'm not fucking you yet, Liv. Trust me, I hate it as much as you do."

"Yeah, but you can take care of business if you need to. I can't."

He laughs and leans in to brush his lips across mine. "I'm not fucking my fist, Liv. I'm waiting for you to be ready. We're in this together."

For some reason, that's just an even bigger turn on.

"One time. Please."

"Absolutely not. You're lucky I've given you the freedom I have." He runs a thumb across my bottom lip, which is an even bigger tease and causes my breath to hitch. "Soon, Sweetheart."

"Not soon enough," I grumble.

All it does is make Jameson laugh, which brings a scowl to my face.

"Aw, come on, baby. Cheer up. We've had a nice few weeks just spending time together, getting to know each other more and with lots of snuggles."

I twirl my finger along his collarbone. His very non-broken collarbone. "We have, but I miss you. The last time we had sex was the day we broke up. Not a great memory. I want to replace it with happier ones."

"We have tons of time for that, Liv. I'm not going anywhere. A few more weeks won't be anything in the grand scheme of things. Trust me. And it won't be a good memory if you start screaming part way through."

A coy smile takes over my face. "I thought getting me to scream was your goal."

Instead of laughing, he sighs heavily. "I mean in agony, Liv. You're not giving yourself enough time to heal all the way. And it's what you need. Fuck, it's what I need. Because I swear I'd kill myself if I did anything to hurt you. So no, we won't be having sex until you're healed and the doctor has cleared it. Because I will, for sure, be asking once you get that nasty cast off."

"It smells. Doesn't it?" My nose crinkles at the thought.

"A little. But it's the nature of having a cast."

I fall to my back and flop my right arm to my side. "I'm just so bored too. How many shows can a person watch? How many books can I read? I want to go back to work. I never thought I'd miss that place, but dammit I do."

"Well. What if you went back for a little? You'd have to be a lot more careful with what you do, and you'd need to accept help, but what if we got you back behind the counter?"

"I'm assuming by help, you mean you'd be coming with me?" I turn my head to face him and cock an eyebrow.

"You bet your fine ass I'll be with you. I told you I'm not letting you out of my sight. Especially not while you're still healing. But that's the deal. Besides, you only have one good arm. How much coffee do you think you can be brewing?"

I turn back to the ceiling and chew on the inside of my cheek. It gets me the hell out of this house, but I'll still have my babysitter. I love Jameson, and love that he's so concerned for me and my wellbeing, but it feels like he's babying me more than just taking care of me.

Still, it wouldn't be terrible to go back to work. At the very least, I can check up on the orders that were supposed to come in for new flavored coffees. And I had wanted to try some new cups too. I could probably work on things like that while there. And getting food is easy enough with one hand.

"Alright, deal. I'd like to go back temporarily, and I'll let you tag along."

He leans over and rests his lips against mine. "Me going was never a negotiation, Liv."

I roll my eyes and push his face from mine with a smirk, getting out of bed.

"What are you doing?" He leans up on an elbow and watches as I struggle to put on a pair of jeans one handed. As much as I hate the help, he usually has to assist me in getting dressed lately.

"Getting ready to go. Come on."

His eyebrows shoot up his face. "Oh, you mean now. I wasn't quite prepared for that. Figured we'd chat with Alina and Mazie first, maybe?"

I shake my head and walk to the edge of the bed for him to button my jeans, which he does without question.

"Alright. Now it is, I guess."

Before we're even through the door of the café, things feel right again. This is how my life is supposed to be, minus the breaks and bruises still riddling my body. Jameson by my side and on my way to my shop in the small-town I love to hate.

Chapter 40
Jameson

While I wasn't expecting Liv to take me up on the offer so immediately, it's clear she needs to be here. There's been a wider smile spanning her face since we got here an hour ago than I've seen in weeks, possibly ever.

Her sisters swarmed her and wrapped her in a tight hug until she said "ow." Holding her arm up in defense, she waved me off when I moved to cross the space.

Everybody in town whose come by has also wrapped her in a hug, many of the older women fawning over her and what a poor dear she is.

Though I've been behind the counter before, the whole café looks different from back here now. It's more than just being on the other side of it, it's the emotions and knowledge that goes into it.

Knowing that Liv is mine and that we're going to be together, knowing that this café is part of my future.

While Liv is busy chatting with one of her old friends who's apparently in town for the weekend, Alina comes over and bumps my shoulder, a wide smile on her face.

"Good to have you back, Jameson."

"Call me Jay. My friends do."

"Are we friends?"

"I hope we'll be family someday soon, Alina. Actually, can you grab Mazie?"

Alina's face pales before turning bright, and she dashes into the back room and pulls her sister out behind her.

"I know this may seem sudden, but I wanted to let you both know that I'm planning on proposing to Liv. Once she's healed up. I have a guy down in the city working on a ring for me now. We'll go down once it's finished and she's out of her cast and gather what I need from there. I'd like to do it there." I glance between the two of them and Mazie opens her mouth to speak, then stops again.

"I plan to talk to Eli and get his blessing too, but since you're both here, I figured I'd ask now while she's distracted."

While Alina has a smile on her face, she bounces on her toes in what I'd think is a nervous energy. I know Mazie's the oldest and probably wants to get married first. But would she deny Liv this?

I remain silent as Mazie looks over at her baby sister. I'm sure a million thoughts and emotions are running through her mind. This young girl who's been through so much, who she had to start mothering while still basically a child herself. But she has to see how much Liv has thrived, how vibrant and bright she is.

When she turns back to me, tears in her eyes, my breath halts and the blood all drops to my feet. But then a light smile graces Mazie's face and my pulse starts again.

"I think that's a great idea, Jameson. We're glad to have you back, and happy that Liv is in the high spirits she's in. It's great to see her like this and we know that it's because of you. So yes, please. We'd love nothing more."

Alina claps and jumps up and down, garnering a narrowed gaze from Liv. She doesn't leave her friend but is now giving us more attention than she had been.

"Okay, now I know you're all close, but you need to keep this a secret. So those smiles on your faces need to go."

They both nod and try to straighten their mouths, but they burst into giggles and hold hands like they're young girls again instead of adult women.

"What's going on over here? You two being nice to Jameson? Mazie?"

Mazie's mouth pops open in horror. "Why am I the one being questioned?"

Liv raises an eyebrow as she wraps her good arm around my waist and snuggles into my side.

"Okay, I get it, but yes, we're being nice to Jameson. We're just happy to have you back, Liv. You've been missed around here." Mazie attaches herself to Liv's other side, and then Alina tags on at the end, and somehow, it's like everybody is hugging me.

When they all let go, the girls burst into a round of giggles before Liv yawns. Which is when I step forward.

"Okay, time to go."

"What? No, it was just one yawn."

"Nope. Time to go." I'm already gathering Liv's things and the keys, planning to drag her out if I have to. I won't take any chances with her, least of all while she's still recovering.

Though she huffs and puts on a show of rolling her eyes, I know she's thankful that I'm being the bad guy. When she gets tired, it tends to hit her like a ton of bricks, and she goes from a little fatigued to wiped out in all of five minutes.

Handing over her purse, I throw my arm around her shoulders, gently so as to not disrupt her collarbone, and pull her into my side, kissing the top of her head.

"Ladies, thanks for the hospitality. We'll be back maybe tomorrow?"

"Yes! Tomorrow. And every day that I can be here, I will be." Liv practically jumps at the suggestion of coming again.

"See you guys then. Sleep, Sibby." Alina runs a hand down the side of Liv's hair, and I know that Liv will listen to Alina more than she wants to listen to me right now. "You're still healing."

Liv nods into Alina's hand and turns to look at me. "I'm ready."

Without another word, I usher her to the car, holding the door open and helping her settle in her seat.

By the time I cross the driver's side, she's curled into position, and if the drive were any longer, she'd surely fall asleep.

Instead of letting her walk back to the house, I scoop her out and into my arms, with her giggling at my show of chivalry.

But she leans her head against my shoulder and leans into me as I carry her into the house. I haven't broached the subject of what I should consider it. Really, I'd like to move and buy something bigger. The real estate in Juniper Grove isn't extensive, but there are bigger houses to be had.

While this one is her first house, and a nice one at that, it's not big enough for my dreams for us.

Marriage and kids. Sure, we'd get by alright with one or two, but it'd be tight. Since money allows, I'd rather go bigger now. I just have to figure out how to bring it up to her.

The first step is probably proposing, letting her know my truest intention is to be with her forever. And all that comes with time. First thing's first, she needs to be back to one hundred percent, and she's getting there slowly day by day.

Three days later, I set a tee time at the golf course with Eli and told Liv the only lie I ever plan to tell her. I left her in the capable hands of her sisters and told her I was going to check on Seth since I'm back.

Instead, I drove twenty minutes out of town to meet Eli, who I see the second I pull into the gravel lot.

I'm not a golfer, and I have no fucking idea if he is either, but this is what guys do. Right? Maybe we can become golfers. It seems like something I'd enjoy.

I park next to him and hop out, heading to the back of the car, though for what purpose, I have no idea. I have no golf clubs in the trunk.

"So, uh, I maybe should have mentioned this, but I don't golf." He runs a hand sheepishly up the back of his head. "At least not in the traditional sense."

"Ha. I don't either. But what's the nontraditional sense? Minigolf?"

A wide smile spans his face as he pulls out a six-pack from the back seat of his car and holds it up. "This is how I golf."

"Sounds like as good a plan as any to me."

He cracks open two beers and hands me one. It's one of the local brews and another damn delicious choice. Who knew Juniper Grove, a dot on the map I'd never heard of before, would have so many amazing things to add to my life?

After a few sips in silence, he looks at me, right in the eyes. "You want to marry Liv. Don't you?"

"How...did the girls? Uh..."

"I pay attention. It's my job to watch over them. And no, they didn't say anything. I kind of figured it'd come up sooner as opposed to later, and then when you asked me to play golf, I figured you either wanted a buddy and that we could be friends, or you wanted to ask. When you had no clubs, I decided on the latter."

"You are a smart motherfucker. Liv has that right."

He laughs and crosses his feet at the ankles.

"Yeah. I wanted your permission to marry Liv. I'd like to take her away after she gets her cast off and propose to her in the city."

"I think that's a great idea. And you don't need my permission. You need hers and hers alone. But know you have my blessing. You're good for her, Jameson. It didn't take me long to see that. You can provide her with a lifestyle she doesn't want to ask for and we can't give her. Things she deserves and needs. Not to mention, you make her happier than I've ever seen her." He looks down at the ground and kicks some pebbles. I can tell he feels guilty about his role in not providing Liv with more, but they all have to know that they can live for themselves a little.

"You guys are so close-knit, sometimes I'm not sure you see that it's okay to be selfish sometimes."

"I'm probably the most selfish of all, living in Pineville City. But I agree and the girls won't hear of it. It's hard when we were brought closer the way we were. But our parents would want more for Liv." Interesting. He didn't seem to hesitate to talk about his parents. Maybe it's not an issue for all of them like I thought.

"They'd probably want more for all of you."

He looks up at the sky and then back at me, readjusting and leaning against the trunk of his car. "Yeah. Maybe. They'd be happy with where I ended up if it wasn't for the path I was on when they died."

"MIT, right?"

He looks at me with narrowed eyes.

"Liv mentioned."

"Oh, so she really went into detail then. Good for her. It's been hard for her to talk about. Alina's the worst. I guess it was that pivotal age for them. Mazie and I have done the best we could, but—" A quick shake of his head is all I as he changes subjects. "Yes. Please, feel like you have my blessing, permission, whatever you want to call it to propose to Liv. I don't give a fuck about pecking order and who's older. If she's found the one, so be it."

"Thanks, man. I really appreciate that. And I hope we can correct our relationship and be...I don't know. Friends? Are you friends with your future brother-in-law or just friendly?"

"I think we can be both. Maybe actually take up golf together?"

"I was thinking the same thing myself. As long as these are part of our rounds." I hold up one of the cans before taking another swig.

"Good, aren't they? A buddy of mine started the company. I like to support him when I can." It's something I've known for a while but is reinforced routinely. Eli's a good man. And it's clear he's had a shitty hand dealt to him and has still done the best he could with what he was given.

"You're a good brother. Liv really admires you. Do you know that?"

His chin hits his chest as he hangs his head. "I do my best. It doesn't feel like it sometimes. But yeah, I know they all look up to me. Why, I'm not sure. I'm nobody great."

"You're the closest thing they have to a dad. And Mazie to a mom, but it's different. You'll walk each of them down the aisle at their wedding."

All the blood leaves his face, and his eyes widen. It seems like a thought he hadn't quite put together. I take it the family tries not to think too much about the lifelong implications of not having their parents around and goes day by day. That's how Liv is, but it seems family wide.

"Yeah. I guess you're right. I'd never thought of that before. Probably because it was never really right in front of us like I guess it is now." He gives me a once-over before nodding firmly.

"You know I'm quite a bit older than your sister. Right? Like closer in age to you than her."

He gives a short laugh and takes a sip of his beer before setting the can to the side and opening another one. "Did you know my dad was nine years older than my mom?"

Shock coils through me and twists around my spine. "No. I never knew that. Like mother like daughter, I guess." Part of me wonders if Liv even knows. Though I suppose I was the one who'd been adamant about the age difference early on and not her.

Eli downs the rest of his beer and pats his legs. "Alright, man. I gotta go grade some papers."

"I thought we were playing golf? Doesn't that take hours?"

"Eh, like I said, had a feeling this was the reason. I'll take you up on a beer any time, though."

"Sounds good to me." Now the only question is what I'll do with the rest of my time. I could probably just go back to Liv and tell her they're doing well and didn't need me for much. But she knows I work more than that. I don't know if I want to head over to Seth and get stuck in the work and then be longer than I planned. I miss my girl. A few weeks alone with her, shortly after several without her, will do that to a person.

Straightening up, Eli extends his hand and pulls me into a hug, clapping his hand against my back. "Alright, brother. I'm going to call you that from now on since you will be soon. Give Liv a hug for me."

"Will do. Thanks again."

He gives a final wave before climbing into his car and starting it up.

I polish off my beer and carry the cans over to a nearby recycling bin, dropping them in and stretching before climbing back into the car.

All the details are in place. The ring is ready, the siblings have given their blessings, and we have a date for Liv to get her cast off. Now all I need is the perfect weekend away with my girl to make her mine forever.

Chapter 41
Liv

The weekend I've been waiting for has finally arrived. Jameson is taking me to the city again. There was so much we didn't get to do or see last time that I need to get to it all in this weekend.

My cast came off a few days ago and everything is healed well. I have a little less range of motion than I did before the accident, but not to the point that I need physical therapy more than a few times to stretch the tight muscles.

The trip is going to be better than the last one also because we won't have a dark cloud hanging over us. Last time, there were conversations to be had. This time? It's just us getting to enjoy some time together and picking up some of his things before he officially moves in with me.

I haven't technically asked him, more of us just picking up where we left off, which was him practically living with me anyway.

He claims he's letting me select some of his suits to keep, but what do I know about fancy suits? They all look incredible on him. So instead, he can pick some.

Though, if he's keeping the apartment, I'd rather he not get rid of any, and just bring a few to my house. Our house. Because as far as I'm concerned, it is *our* house. I want him there with me, all the time. I gave him back his key, which he had sneakily left on the railing of the porch during our last fight. Thankfully, Eli found it that night and brought it in. We're some of the only people who lock our doors, small-town vibes and all that. But with our history, it's engrained in us.

A nervous energy has overtaken me and my leg bounces incessantly. I don't know what I'm so anxious about. We're on solid footing, we're happily in love, possibly more now than we were before, if only because we're allowing ourselves to be.

"Liv. Everything is fine. Calm down." Jameson rests his hand on my thigh while he drives.

"I don't know why I'm nervous." Part of me feels like I'm picking up on something coming from Jay, but what would he have to be nervous about? Unless...

"You, uh. You didn't hook up with anybody while we were apart. Did you?" I look at him with large round eyes, hoping that the answer is what I want it to be.

When he flips his eyes to me like I've lost my mind, I know it is. "Of course not. What kind of question is that?"

"I don't know...you seem a little off yourself and I wasn't sure if maybe there was something that happened that you were thinking about and didn't know how to bring it up."

"No, Liv. I want *you* and only you. At some point, I probably would have moved on, but definitely not that quickly. You were all I could think about." He looks at me, then the road, then back again, his gaze narrowing each time he glances my way. "You didn't either. Did you?"

I squeeze his hand in mine and laugh. "Didn't even cross my mind." Leaning my head against the headrest, I look at him. "I love you. You know that, right?"

A smile breaks across his face, and he pulls my knuckles to his lips. "I love you too."

"I think I'm just worried you're going to be there and get cold feet about moving. Change your mind and realize that you can't give up the city life after all." There. Now I've at least voiced one of my concerns.

"Two things. One, I'm not giving it up, because we're keeping the apartment and we'll come down once or twice a month to romp around and have fun. And two, I'm gaining something much more important and valuable than a place to live. I'm gaining you." He turns to me, and I find sincerity sweeping through his eyes.

"If you're sure..."

"I am, Liv. I promise. I wouldn't make this arrangement, these promises to you, if I didn't mean them. Besides, we're not losing the apartment, we're just not living there. We'll have two places to live and come visit whenever you want to."

"What if that's every weekend?" It's entirely possible, at least in the nice weather.

"Then we'll come every weekend. You seem to be missing the point that it's to make you happy, Liv."

Heat creeps up my face as he points out my inability to grasp what he's truly doing. Nobody has ever had my happiness as their primary focus before.

I nestle into my seat and prepare for the rest of the drive. We're still about an hour out, so I can get a quick nap in to prepare myself for whatever's on tap for today.

Jay's hand runs up and down my thigh, squeezing my hip before settling there.

He drives straight to his underground parking garage and pulls into what I learned last time is his assigned spot. We take the elevator up in silence, the eagerness causing me to bounce on my toes.

Jameson smiles as he shakes his head and looks down at the ground. I know he thinks I'm being ridiculous, but there was so much I didn't get to experience last time.

The second he opens the door, I cross the threshold and take a deep breath. It smells like Jameson. It smells like home. It's exactly how I remember it, the large open space of the kitchen and living room, with windows that overlook the river and the rest of the amazing view.

"Wow. That view never gets old. Does it?"

"Nope, it certainly doesn't." The way he says it, from behind me and with a touch of strain to his voice, causes me to turn around. To find him staring right at my ass.

"I was talking about the view out the *window,* Jameson. Not my body."

He lifts one shoulder but continues to stare at me. "You know what I love about bringing you here? Is that I know we won't have any interruptions when I fuck you. No phone calls, nobody ringing the bell. Nothing."

A few quick strides and he's standing in front of me, cupping my face with one hand and my ass with the other. He runs his thumb under my eye as he looks down at me intently.

When Jameson holds me, I feel safer than I ever have in my life. I rest my cheek against his chest and close my eyes, letting the steady sound of his heart calm my own.

"Deep breaths, baby. We have a busy weekend ahead of us. And no heels this time."

"I didn't even pack any."

"Good. Though you may want a pair for tomorrow. I'm taking you to a Broadway play."

My jaw drops, and I lean back with my arms around his waist to keep me from falling over. "You're joking."

"Not even a little. We can probably see anything. We'll try the ticket offices at whichever you want and see what we can find."

"Isn't it more expensive that way?"

"You let me worry about that. Okay?"

"Then I guess we get to go shopping today." I stick out my tongue and wiggle my shoulders in excitement.

Seeing a play has been at the top of my list for ages, but it's not something I've ever told Jameson. Somehow, like so many other things, he just knows what I need.

Chapter 42
Jameson

I'm more nervous than I thought I'd be today. Liv's ring sits firmly in my pants pocket. She fell asleep early after an afternoon of shopping, and I was able to meet Michael downstairs to finally buy it from him.

Last night, while Liv slept draped across my lap and I played with her hair, I couldn't stop looking at it. Any time she fidgeted, I'd panic and pop the box closed, shoving it under my pillow, but she slept straight through.

Her face is bright and wide, like it has been since we walked into The Gershwin. She was a little overwhelmed with all the options and told me to just choose one. *Wicked* is still playing, and it's something I know Liv will enjoy. Who doesn't love a musical rendition of The Wizard of Oz? A slightly different telling, but who wouldn't enjoy it?

Liv is literally sitting on the edge of her seat, her head tilted to the side and her eyes wide with wonder. We're only in the first half of the show and this ring is starting to burn a hole through my pocket. I want nothing more than to ask Liv to be mine forever. And she looks fucking incredible in her tight black dress and heels. Which makes today all the more special.

After our matinee, I plan to take her to dinner and then to the top of the Empire State Building. But I won't propose to her until we're back in my apartment. I don't do showy, grand gestures. It's just not my style, and I don't really think Liv would care about all the people around.

In fact, the only hesitation I've had is that her family *isn't* around. But this is something I'm doing to be selfish. I want to ask privately, where it's just Liv and myself, no distractions, no interruptions.

Sometimes I feel like Liv's life is so busy with friends and family that she forgets there can be quiet moments. And she and I need those. The few weeks when it was just the two of us at her house while she was injured were some of the best of my life because I got to be with her and her alone. I love how close she is with her siblings; it's really awe inspiring and something that I hope our kids have someday, but she and I need our private time too.

I'm a private person and keep a lot of things close to the vest. I've opened with Liv and even with her family, but it's exhausting having people around all the time.

Alina's nightmares haven't gotten better. She doesn't call Liv as much, but it's clear to me she's still struggling. That conversation we had a few months ago doesn't seem to have been worthwhile. I begged her to seek help from a therapist. It's something I had to do when my mom passed away. I too had trouble sleeping afterward.

But it's clear she hasn't sought help of any kind. And now, because she doesn't want to bother me and Liv, she suffers alone. The circles under her eyes are dark and deep.

I never expected to find a person I love and taking a whole family with her, but that's what you get with Liv. Siblings. They're a unit. And to truly be in love with Liv, which I am, means worrying about her family just like she would.

Liv claps next to me, drawing my attention back to the matter at hand. Her face is alight with excitement, and it makes a wide smile span my face. The lights come on, and I realize it's intermission. The day is floating by faster than I want it to.

"Oh my God, Jameson. This is amazing. Thank you so much for bringing me. I can't even begin to tell you how much this means to me."

Reaching out, I tuck a curl behind her ear. "I'm glad you're enjoying yourself. I wanted to make this weekend perfect for you. After all you've been through recently, you deserve it. And you look sexy as hell, which is a perk for me."

Her face pinks slightly. "Do I not always look sexy for you?"

"Oh, you do. But this is extra. With that tight dress and heels? Come on now."

A wicked smile pulls up the corners of her lips and she knows exactly what she's doing and asking.

"Now's a good time to use the bathroom. We have the next half still to go. And there's a bar if you want a drink." Changing the subject will keep my cock from pressing against my zipper. I can't wait to get her home and tear this dress right off her body.

"Oh, I do have to pee. But no drink. God, it's just so amazing. And their voices! Incredible. Alina's going to be so jealous. We'll have to bring her to see a play sometime."

I lean forward and press my lips to hers. "Anything you want."

We take our time stretching and using the restrooms while people mill about and talk about how wonderful the show is. When the lights dim as a request to take our seats, Liv grabs my hand and practically drags me back to our spot.

This spoiling her is something I'm quickly getting used to, and I can't wait to do it for the rest of my life.

Chapter 43

Liv

Wicked is truly amazing. I'm jealous that Jameson has been able to come to a play anytime he wants for the last several years, though he swears he hasn't seen that many.

The whole day has been filled with things I'd want to do, and I haven't stopped smiling.

Jay's even carrying around my bags from the Gershwin gift shop. I couldn't very well return home after seeing a play without memorabilia. He won't tell me where we're going now, but we're in a cab instead of walking because he says there's no way I can do it in my heels.

He's being cryptic, but since the whole day has been incredible, I won't question it.

"So, is this whole weekend about me, or are we going to do some things *you* want to do?" I hook my arms around his and rest my chin on his shoulder as the cab lurches forward.

"Spoiling you *is* what I want to do. Making you happy, that's the greatest feeling in the world." My heart flutters at his sincerity, something I've found increasingly sweet since my accident.

But this weekend is going above and beyond. We're here to gather his things and should be back at his apartment packing. Instead, we're gallivanting around, doing things I want.

"You're not changing your mind about moving to Juniper Grove. Right?"

"Of course not. Why would I?"

"We're just not spending any time getting your things together."

"That's what tomorrow is for." He turns to me with a smile and loops his arm around my shoulders, pulling me against his side and kissing the top of my head.

The cab pulls to the side and stops, announcing the fare, and I look out my window. My heart stops as I see the Empire State Building.

"Come on, we're going to the top."

"Jameson, I don't have the shoes for climbing."

"It's an elevator. Though, it can be a lot of standing. I'll give you a piggyback if need be."

"In this dress? Are you crazy?" The dress is far too tight for a piggyback. My whole ass would hang out the bottom.

"Well, should we not go?" He turns his upper half to look me dead on. There's not an ounce of annoyance in his demeanor or tone. He truly wants to do what I want, even if that's to turn around and go back to his apartment right now.

"No, I'll tough it out. I've always wanted to go to the top." I glance out the window again as he leans around me and pulls the handle on the door to swing it open.

"I know." He kisses right against my ear as he ushers me from the taxi.

We wait in line, pressed against one another, Jameson's chest flush with my back and his arms tight around my middle. I lean my head back against his collarbone and we sway to music that doesn't exist.

"How are you feeling? I probably should have taken your soreness into account," he mostly grumbles to himself.

"I'm fine, Jay. Nothing hurts. My feet will by the end of the night, but my shoulder and wrist are fine. They're barely even being used, and my ribs are all healed up nicely. I promise."

"Foot massage when we get back to the apartment." Even better. The last time he gave me a foot massage, I fell right asleep, something I'm sure will happen again tonight because I'm already feeling exhausted. But I can't tell him that because he'll want to take me right home to rest.

The line inches forward enough that I can see the elevator and excitement swirls in my chest. I can't wait to get to the top. It's so iconic. I'm sure Jameson isn't as excited to do all the touristy things, but I'm happy he's willing to do them with me and for me.

We're able to make it up in this round of filling the elevator and I bounce on my toes the whole ride.

The top is everything I dreamed it would be. It's windy and chilly but the view is well worth it. Even at night. Maybe even better, because you can see everything brightly lit and it looks magical.

I wrap my arms around myself for warmth and Jameson takes off his sport coat, hanging it over my shoulders and kissing the top of my head. The Statue of Liberty is beautifully alit, the gold shining through in such a way that it looks like fire.

"Wow." I turn in the light hold Jameson has on my waist. "Jameson, this is amazing. Thank you for bringing me here. For this whole day. It's been incredible since the moment we woke up."

His gray eyes glint in the surrounding lights as a smile spreads across his face. "Of course, Sweetheart. I want you to see everything you want. Experience all you want to experience."

"Well, this has been the best day of my life. And I'm so happy I get to do it all with you."

A shiver wracks through my body, and he rubs his hands up and down my biceps. "Why don't we get you back to the apartment to rest those feet and warm up a bit."

"That sounds nice." As much as I'd stay here and keep looking around, I'm cold and my feet are killing me. Heels are never a good idea for more than looks.

We wait our turn for the down elevator and take another taxi back to the apartment.

I'm standing in front of the window, barefoot with a blanket wrapped around me as Jameson makes some fresh coffee to help warm me up. This window is my favorite place to be in this apartment, looking out over the city and skyline. It's beautiful, day or night.

I'm so mesmerized, I barely hear him return to the living room until he says my name. "Liv."

When I turn around, he's down on one knee, a box in his hand. The blanket pools around my feet as my hands fly to my mouth. "Jay." It comes out a whisper as a lump lodges in my throat and my eyes fill with tears.

"I love you, Liv. I've known that for a long time. Even though I didn't want to find you, there you were, and it was impossible not to fall for you. You're the most amazing woman I've ever met, and I would be the luckiest man in the world if you'd marry me."

"Yes. Of course, yes." My breath stalls when he opens the ring box, and a large oval diamond sits on a band encrusted with smaller diamonds. It glints off every light possible. "Oh my God, Jay. It's beautiful."

"It's barely enough for you." He slips the ring on my finger, kisses my knuckles and stands, pulling me into his chest.

With one finger, he tilts my chin up and presses his lips to mine. I throw my arms around his shoulders and jump to wrap my legs around his waist.

His hands grab my ass, and he pulls me closer to him, opening my mouth with his tongue. Setting me down at the back of the couch, he pushes between my shoulder blades so my chest is against the top of the cushions and I can look out the window.

His palms slide up the back of my thighs, pushing my dress up on the way and exposing my ass, which he gives a firm slap. "So delicious, Liv. I'm a lucky man."

I shiver as I hear the zipper of his pants sliding down and his fingers slip along my soaking pussy before dipping them inside. Lurching forward, I grab the cushions as he starts working his fingers feverishly inside me.

My teeth bite into the fabric in front of me as he brings me unbridled pleasure. His hand twists in my curls and he pulls back so I'm pushing up on my hands and I can glance back to see his erection free in front of him. "Jay."

"What do you want, Sweetheart?" He continues pumping his fingers, curling them just right.

"I want you to fuck me. Hard."

Without another word, he removes his fingers and slams into me in one full thrust. I cry out and arch my back as my head tips up. "Fuck, Liv. So wet and tight."

He starts thrusting into me, hard and fast, just like I love. My whole body shifts with the force, my breasts rubbing against the top of the couch. When I can keep my eyes open, I can look right out the window and see all the lights shining. It's a truly magical experience.

His hands wrap around my hips, and he uses them to push me forward and back, each slam causing me to whine. He repeats the motions over and over again, each time bringing me closer and closer to pure bliss.

"Jay. Please."

He pulls out, the opposite of what I want, and gently flips me over the couch so I'm lying on it instead of bent over it. Walking around the couch, he kicks off his pants and boxer briefs, leaving himself in just a shirt and tie. When he starts to loosen the tie, I reach out to stop him.

"Leave it."

He smiles and lowers himself over me, immediately burying his cock deep inside me as my hands wrap to his shoulders and my head tips back with a moan.

Cupping my ass with one hand, he drives into me, his breaths coming in short spurts.

My fingers knot into the front of shirt and wrap into his tie. Closer, I need him closer.

I pull him down on top of me so his lips crash against mine. It's heated and fiery as he pumps into me. Every tip of his hips lights a new fire inside my body until I'm an inferno of need and burning desire.

When his tongue slips between my lips, it's all over for me, and I moan into his mouth, tightening around him as I pull him impossibly close, his lips bruising my own.

He pulls his mouth from mine to groan before dropping his forehead against mine, breathing heavily as he slows his hips.

We stay in this embrace for a few minutes, forehead to forehead, regaining our normal breathing pattern before he brushes his lips against mine. "I love you."

"I love you too."

We clean up and change, Jameson into a pair of low hung sweatpants and me into one of his large t-shirts, before settling back on the couch. It's early still, with plenty of the night ahead of us, but I'm tired.

"Feet up." He pats his legs and pulls my feet into his lap. The second he starts massaging my right foot, I moan and settle back into the corner of the couch. He laughs and stops to tuck me in with the throw before going back to his task.

The thumb of my left hand finds the large diamond that now sits proudly on my ring finger. It feels different, wearing a ring where one wasn't before. And it's heavy. But it's perfect. I don't care about the size or shape or any of the Cs involved in picking a diamond. I care about the fact that Jameson loves me enough to move to Juniper Grove and wants to marry me.

Somehow, the man who was a huge douchebag the first time we met, is going to be my husband, the love of my life. The café and small town, both of which I still hate to love and love to hate, brought me my forever.

Epilogue
Liv

Jameson and I decide not to wait to get married, having a small ceremony with some close friends and my siblings in the spring. We don't see a reason to put it off.

After we drove back from the city, all three of my siblings were waiting for me out on the front lawn of my house, with champagne, orange juice, and Jameson's favorite muffins. It was their way of being involved and congratulating us.

The whole town found out pretty quickly. Word travels fast and the rock on my finger does a lot of talking. Even three months later, we still receive congratulations on what feels like a daily basis.

It's part of the small-town charm.

The day of our wedding isn't filled with butterflies like most say. If anything, I'm antsy, ready to make Jameson mine forever.

Everything is perfect. We host the wedding at our house, because we don't see a need to be extravagant. Or at least, I don't. The wedding isn't a huge deal to me, and not having my parents around makes me want it that much more lowkey. Instead, I've told Jameson he can plan the honeymoon he wants, anywhere he wants to take me, no holds barred.

He begrudgingly agreed. Mostly because he didn't have a lot of people to invite, and I was able to convince him that small is better because the people leave sooner.

Alina is catering and making the cake, something she insists on surprising me with and won't even let me into the kitchen the week of the wedding.

Mazie is handling all the small details, and Eli knows a guy who can DJ and bartend. Not that we need too much, since it's such a small group of us, but I appreciate their input all the same.

Everybody is coming together for me, and I love them for it.

After my accident, that changed tremendously, but he's still an outsider to our little group.

As I sit contemplating my fairly simple sheath wedding dress, I glance over at Mazie, who has tears in her eyes.

"Mazie. Are you sure you're okay that I'm getting married before you?" It's something we've talked about extensively because I'm not willing to let there be any hard feelings. I'll postpone it for years, if need be.

"Of course, Liv. It's a happy day. But I'm sad they're not here to see it. They'd be so proud of the woman you've become." She takes a few steps closer and runs her thumb across my cheek as her tears spill over.

"Stop crying or you're going to make me cry and then I'll have to redo my makeup."

She looks at the sky and blinks a few times, trying to will the tears away. "You're right. And I'll have to redo mine. But know I'm happy for you, baby sister. Today is a great day, and Jameson is a good man."

"The best."

Eli and Alina walk in laughing and quickly take a state of the room, sobering quickly. "Everybody okay?" Eli puts his hand on my back as he asks.

We all look at one another and nod, as though our sibling bond allows us to share what's troubling us without words. Eli shoves his hands in his pockets and rocks back on his heels as he lets out a puff of air.

"They'd be happy, Liv. And proud. Of all of us." He always speaks with such authority when he talks about our parents and how they'd feel or handle certain situations. I like to think being the oldest, he really knows, that he learned enough about them and their likes and interests, but he was just a kid himself when they died.

"It's just hard, with them not here to see this big day. They won't be here for any of us." I glance around at my siblings and take in their looks of defeat. It's the same for all of us; I'm just going first.

"We have each other. That's what's important. And it's a huge day. Let's not let their absence weigh too heavily on that." Mazie has taken back the role of mother and not sister, straightening with her words and running her hands down her dress.

With a nod, we all crawl out of the dark hole we were just in.

"You look beautiful, Sibby."

"You really do, babiest sister." We all laugh at Eli's joke. He's always called me the babiest sister since we're all baby sisters to him. It's something he started when we were kids, and like all the nicknames, it just stuck.

Everybody suddenly a gets renewed vigor, and we go about the last-minute details of the day. I'm walking down the aisle myself. Not as any sort of diss to Eli, as he's been a great brother and the closest thing to a father figure that I could have. But he needs to remember he's my brother first.

Jameson and I chose to go sans Best Man and Maid of Honor as well. Everything is small, with just some friends on our lawn and a Justice of the Peace.

The whole thing goes by in a flash, and I barely even remember putting rings on our fingers and saying I dos. The one thing that pulls me from my haze is the kiss.

Our guests hoot and holler, shouting their congratulations and blowing bubbles at us as we laugh, me still tipped backward as his lips leave mine and spread into a bright smile.

None of it matters and none of it's my focus. Jameson is. He's everything I never knew I wanted or needed. And now he's mine forever.

Epilogue
Jameson

Liv and I have been back from our honeymoon and living in her house for five weeks. We still get routine congratulations, even though the wedding was over a month ago.

We've started house hunting too, as I want something a little bigger for us and our future family.

I'm thankfully back to work. Hanging with Liv at the café has been fun, but it's not my scene. One of the local hotels wanted help streamlining their costs, and Seth sang my praises, so I've been working over there. It's nice for Liv and me to get our time apart to work, and then come home together.

While the time we were glued at the hip was nice, and I was able to be protective over Liv in her injured state, it's nice to be able to talk about our days instead of already knowing how they went.

Most days, I make a trip to the café for lunch together. That's what I'm on my way to do now.

The second I walk in, something is amiss. There's a man standing at the counter, and he looks desperate.

"You've been *gone* for years, Cameron. That's why. Only my friends and siblings can call me Liv. That doesn't include you anymore." Liv's arms are crossed firmly over her chest. I'm not sure who this Cameron guy is, but he's rubbing Liv the wrong way.

My senses are heightened and all I can think about is making Liv more comfortable, so I walk over and wrap my arm around her, pulling her into my side. It doesn't work exactly how I want, as she keeps her arms crossed tightly, but she does lean into me, and I can feel her muscles loosen under my hands.

"Everything okay here?" Clearly it isn't, but somebody needs to spill the beans before I start making assumptions.

"Yes, he was just leaving." There's a forcefulness to Liv's tone, as though that's not what's actually happening, but she's trying to force it to be the course of action.

"Actually, I'm waiting for Alina."

"I told you, she's not coming out." This comes through mostly gritted teeth.

I look back and forth between the two of them briefly. They know each other, but the question is how. Liv has grumbled a few times about somebody being back, but she refuses to go into details. Instead of pressing, I let her be because I know she'll come out with it when she's ready.

Tightening my arm around her, I extend a hand. "Hi. I'm Jameson."

"Cameron." He places his hand in mine, and we shake firmly. I notice the once-over he gives me, taking in the suit as his eyes widen. But it's not until his gaze lands on Liv's finger as it rests against my chest that his color changes.

Clearing his throat, he juts his chin forward. "Congratulations."

Liv turns away from him, facing the back wall, and tightens her grip on my shirt. Whatever happened between these two is a big deal. "Thanks, man. Listen, I don't know what's going on here, but you're upsetting my girl, and I can't have that right now."

"I know, I'm sorry. I'll go. Liv, please, tell Alina I'll be back tomorrow. And the next day. I'll be back every single day until she talks to me."

Liv flips back around, her freshly pink streaks flying through the air with the force of her turn. "She's never going to talk to you, Cameron. You should just go back to wherever you came from. She's moved on, and she's not interested."

"Five minutes, Liv. All I need is five minutes."

"Good luck with that." I try to keep my grasp on her as she pushes off me, but it's no use. She's gone and walking through the black door into oblivion.

I look after Liv for a moment before turning back to Cameron, then back to the door and back again. I don't know who this guy is, but I feel kind of bad for him. This group can be hard to break through. I, of all people, should know. "What can I do to help you out?"

"I just need five minutes to talk to her. That's it."

"Listen, I don't know who you are, what your deal is, but I know with these girls it can be tough to break through their defenses. Trust me. I'll see if there's anything I can do." First, I plan to find out the story of who he is and what he's doing. I'll do my best to get him time, but I'm not putting my girl, or her sisters, at risk.

But nothing about this guy gives off dangerous vibes. I get to know a lot of people in my line of work and often have to judge them from the get-go. I'm getting nothing but sincerity from him and his need to talk to Alina.

He makes no move to leave, so I clear my throat. That gets him to shake out of the reverie he's in and he backs up. "Tell the girls I'll be back tomorrow. All I want is five minutes of Alina's time. That's it."

"I'll tell them."

With a curt nod, he leaves the café.

It takes all of two seconds for Liv to burst back through the door, pacing behind the counter. She rakes her fingers through her hair.

I catch her mid-stride and put my hands on her shoulders. "Sweetheart. Who was that?"

Her eyes are wide and wild. "Alina's ex-boyfriend. This isn't good, Jay."

An ex-boyfriend? I guess that makes sense. But why is Alina so against seeing him? Something bad must have happened between them.

"Well, prepare yourselves, because he plans to come back."

She groans and crashes her head against my chest. "Why is he back? Why did he have to come back?"

I wrap my arms around her and pull her into my chest. While I don't know what happened, when they dated, or any details, it doesn't seem like good news that he's back in town.

The End
Alina's story comes next!

COMING September 2023

The following is an unedited preview and subject to change.

Chapter 1

Alina

Laughter fills the otherwise quiet café as Liv has me gripping my sides. She's always been able to make me see the light, to find the good in the bad. I know it's not that way for her, but she can do it for me. And it makes me love her all the more. She may be my sister, but she's also my best friend.

When she suddenly stops, all color draining from her face and her mouth hanging open, my heart crashes to the ground. Something bad is happening behind me and I'm scared to turn around.

"Hey Liv." *That voice.*

Suddenly her expression makes sense.

"You have a lot of nerve coming in here like everything is fine, Cameron." Her tone is stern and angry as she speaks for me.

I flinch at the mention of his name. Instead of turning around, I place a hand on Liv's arm, drawing her attention, and lightly tilt my head toward the kitchen. My safe place, my solace.

She gives the slightest nod and I walk away, without turning around and seeing him. Because as much as I tell myself I moved on, that I've forgotten about him, the scars on my heart ache at the deep timber of his voice.

"Alina." My shoulders hunch as my name rolls off his tongue. I used to love the way he said it, the way he could make it sound like the sweetest song. Now, it only brings me pain.

"Don't you dare talk to her." It's the last thing I hear as I disappear through the door to the kitchen.

Once through it, my hand flies to my chest and I try to gulp down air. My heart is pounding against my sternum and I can't take a deep breath no matter how hard I try.

"Leen?" Liv pokes her head in right as I double over, one hand on my knee while the other tries to contain my heart. "Oh, Alina." Her arm drapes over my shoulder and she pulls into her side.

"What...is he...doing here?"

"Well, he's not here any more. I made sure of that. But, I don't know. He said he wanted to see you, that he was back." Back? What does that mean? For good? For the day? I can't handle either.

"Why?"

"Your guess is as good as mine. He may have been like another brother to me but you were obviously a lot closer with him." At one point I was pretty sure he *would* be a brother to her. We were so set, so strong, I was sure we were going to get married. That all changed when he left.

"I can't handle him being back, Liv."

"Listen, I know he was your first love, your big love, but you moved on. Right? You've dated. Hell, you were with Steve for two years."

Steve was just a bandaid on a gaping wound. Yes, he was sweet and kind and wanted to be with me, but his love never had a chance to compare to what I had with Cameron once upon a time.

"It's not about moving on Liv, it's not about still having feelings for him. He *broke* me when he left. It took far too long for me to heal from that. Nothing good can come from him being back. There's nothing left between us, no torches still held. It's just going to stir up bad feelings. It already is."

Tipping my head back against the door, I stare at the ceiling, willing away the torrent of tears threatening to fill my eyes. It's been ten years since Cameron left. I've moved on, I've dated, came close to getting engaged once. But the way he left, the memories, the times we shared, seeing him again, hearing his voice has torn open those wounds.

He was everything to me for so many years. We may have been young, only eighteen when he left, but we were so in love. Nothing has quite compared. And I was okay with that, I've come to terms with the fact that I may never find somebody who makes me feel the way Cameron did.

"Why is here, Liv?" The thought is going to plague my mine for as long as he's around.

"I don't know. Maybe to see his folks? Aren't they still local?"

"Yeah, but has he not seen them in ten years? I can't imagine that's the case. He has to have been coming back here for years and made sure to stay hidden. Why now?" What's changed? Is it something about being a decade? Is there some sort of reunion I'm not aware of that he's here for and wanted to see me before being around all those people?

There has to be a reason and it can't just be to upturn my life. I've already let him do that once, when he left. I can't let him do it again.

"I couldn't tell you, Leen. Really. I wish I knew, that I had some sort of information or inkling, but I don't. All I know is that he seemed adamant. He said he'd be back."

"Fuck my life. I'm never leaving this kitchen again." And I'd gladly stay here forever. I can sleep on the benches, I don't need to be home. Maybe the nightmares will abate when I'm in my happy place.

But is it still happy, knowing he's going to be out there waiting?

My fingers tingle at my sides with the need to move, to do something, to *cook*. "I'm going to whip up some muffins."

"Leen, don't get too crazy."

"I won't, Sibby." Using Liv's long standing nickname brings me a sense of comfort that I desperately want right now. "I just...I need to do something. You know that nervous energy."

"Want to stay at my place tonight?" She's anticipating a nightmare from his return. It's not the craziest though because I wouldn't be surprised if I had one.

"No. I'll be fine. I don't want to impose on you and Jameson. He's been kind enough to share you if I have a nightmare, I don't need to stay with you too."

"Well if this stirs up any memories or bad dreams, you just let me know. Don't hesitate to call."

I glance at her and don't answer.

She takes my shoulders in her hands and turns me to face her. "He may be my husband but you are my sister and I love you and if you need me, you are to call me so I can be there for you. Understood?"

I can't meet her gaze but I nod as I stare down at the tiled floor beneath our feet. It makes me feel so weak that I lose such control of my mind while I'm asleep. I'd rather just not sleep. And I do try, but eventually my body fails me and I pass out.

Jameson tried to have a conversation with me, urging me to seek help. But I can't trust a stranger with my problems.

In fact I have a hard time trusting anybody, and a large reason for that is because of the man who just stopped into my cafe entirely uninvited.

With a squeeze of my shoulders, Liv walks back through the swinging door and out to the floor. It's almost lunch time which is busy. Enough that some weeks we have our extra help come in.

The second she's gone, I straighten up and do what I do best. Put Cameron out of my mind and focus on baking.

Acknowledgements

What an amazing journey it's been to get here. With that, comes many thanks.

To my amazing husband and children:

Another book, another thank you. I still cannot begin to truly show or explain my gratitude for all that you do and all the ways you continue to support me on this incredible journey.

I truly could not do a single aspect of this without you. Having you by my side every step of the way means so much to me.

I love you!

To my amazing duo; AK, RL:

You are my rock solid team. There for any question, any confusion, any help I need, I know you're there. It's amazing to have found not just great writing partners, but friends.

To my awesome beta readers:

Thank you so much for coming on late in the game. And especially for loving this story as much as I do! You've been so helpful and I can't wait to share more work with you.

To my awesome PA, Jennifer Webb:

Thank you for being my biggest cheerleader! I could not do this without your constant support!

To my incredible street team:

Thank you all for you continued support of me and my work. It's amazing to have readers who enjoy my work enough to want to promote it for others to read. I'm truly thankful for you all.

To my amazing editors Mackenzie and Beth:

This book would not be what it is without you and your input. Thank you for helping me learn how to be a better writer, adjusting my words, and most importantly, keeping my voice my own. And especially for your beautiful words as you read through it.

Thank you to the amazing **Fine's Fine Designs** for my stunning cover!

To my ARC team: Your time and effort does not go unnoticed. Thank you for reading my novel before it hit the public and for your gracious reviews. I know it's not always easy to find the words, but it's all so appreciated.

And most importantly, to the readers:

Thank you for taking a chance on a small author like myself. I know it can be difficult to see a new name and say "hey let me try that" but it is so beyond appreciated, I cannot begin to find the words. I write because it's my passion, but I publish because I want to share my words with all of you. I hope you enjoyed reading it, as much as I enjoyed writing it.

About the Author

Shayna Astor is a romance author who loves writing sweet love stories, with a lot of spice. When she's not writing, she's probably watching The Office with a cup of coffee, spending time with her kids, or playing video games with her husband.

Stalk me for all the latest updates, teasers for upcoming novels, giveaways, and all the goods on what's coming next!

facebook.com/groups/shaynascoffeecorner

instagram.com/shayna.astor.author/

tiktok.com/@shayna.astor.author

amazon.com/stores/Shayna-Astor/author/B09LWXLVMG

Instagram @shayna.astor.author

TikTok @shayna.astor.author

Facebook Group Shayna's Coffee Corner

Website www.shaynaastor.com